I0456768

Stonewall Against The Vulture Men

A Shattered Moon Novel

Joseph Browning

Text Copyright © 2019 by Joseph Browning

Published by Expeditious Retreat Press
Cover by Vivid Covers
Edited by Elizabeth VanZwolle

For information regarding Joseph Browning's novels and to subscribe to his mailing list, see his website at https://www.joseph-browning.com

To follow Joseph on Twitter: https://twitter.com/Joseph_Browning

To follow Joseph on Facebook: https://www.facebook.com/joseph.browning.52

To follow Joseph on MeWee: https://mewe.com/i/josephbrowning

By Joseph Browning

SHATTERED MOON NOVELS: STONEWALL SERIES
Stonewall Against the Rat Men
Stonewall Against the Vulture Men
Stonewall Against Las Vegas
Stonewall Against the Center Sea

Chapter One

Our Story So Far

Everything was fine until there was a shareholder rebellion amongst the vulture men of Waukegan. I know, I know, a venue of vulture men do not a corporation make, and they really don't own shares, per se. But let's be honest, if you had to choose between "inability to pick a tribal chief" and "shareholder rebellion" knowing that the vulture men living in the penthouse of the Lancaster Building built their entire society around an ancient corporation's organizational chart, which one would you choose? Thought so.

The vulture men of Waukegan rule over approximately one hundred square miles, north of the great ruins of Chicago. They're paid tribute by all the communities in the region in exchange for their protection...which includes protection from the vulture men themselves. The vulture men aren't so much rulers as a band of aerial Mafioso. If you don't pay them what they say you owe them, they fly over your community and drop rocks on your head. Simple. Effective.

It isn't all bad. If an insane band of cannibals suddenly shows up outside your walls, you can call in the vulture men and they'll show up and drop rocks on them instead of you. Of course, you pay extra for that service, but they are bound by their own pride and traditions. If the vulture men are thugs, they are willing to be your thugs as long as you keep paying them. And if they make a deal, they keep it. If you have to make an arrangement with the mob, better they are more like a Vito Corleone-style operation instead of a Scarface-style one.

The vulture men live in a twenty-eight-story building called the Lancaster Building. They boarded up the top three levels for themselves, skeletonized the middle levels down to the structural girders, and left the bottom ten levels for their ground force of horcs. Horcs are bipedal warthog men with the horns of an antelope. The typical horc is over six feet tall and packed with muscle under their porcine exteriors. Found in the ruins and rubble under the shattered moon, horcs are an unfriendly bunch that would rather kill and eat you than talk. The vulture men recruit and keep a cadre of horcs as extra added muscle and home defense. If a community decides that they don't want to pay up and hunker down so the vulture men can't drop rocks on them, the horcs are used to convince the recalcitrant citizens that paying the vulture men is in everyone's best interests. Not that the horcs are used in that capacity often; the threat of foul piggy rampage is enough of a deterrent that most pay up reliably. The horcs spend most of their time scavenging in the ruins, hunting for sport and food, and bringing back gifts for their bosses.

The vulture men also have a contingent of flying vulture dogs, mangy-looking winged hounds with vulture heads. They use them as clean-up troops; after the vulture men kill or wound most of their land-based enemies with falling rocks, they send in their dogs to finish them off. For anyone on the battlefield that isn't ready to be lunch, the vulture dogs have a horrid hiss that both injures and stuns, sort of like a taser. Kept in kennels on the roof of the Lancaster Building, I would hate to be their dog walker.

All of the vulture men wear what can only be described as homespun business suits, typically dark blues and grays. They also loop a brightly dyed strip of red cloth about their necks in a poor imitation of a tie. As I said, they went whole hog with the corporate theme.

They even take their names from an employee list they had found for the Lancaster & Penn Real Estate Development company. They don't understand what the names mean, so they use them as titles. For example, whenever a vulture man is promoted in rank, he takes on a new name higher up on the company's organizational chart; and their chief, or rather CEO, is always called the William Howard Spence III, regardless which vulture man is chief.

This distribution of status and their accompanying name-titles was the crux of the shareholder rebellion. The William Howard Spence III was old and died, and the two vulture men who wanted his position were equally matched in ability.

Neither could sway the Board of Directors (no really, there are eight vulture men on the board who decide which vulture men occupy the top three positions) to their side. The Preston Hammond Wolcott, Esq. and the Hayden Miles Dannavant wouldn't back down on their claims for CEO, creating a rift in their society as lower vulture men took sides.

How do I know all this? Don't I live thirteen miles away in Deeplac? Well, the last time I met with the vulture men, I was handing over a rat man I'd captured in exchange for two tribute favors, little pieces of orange plastic "notarized" with scratched symbols on them that can be used in place of the normal monthly tribute payments. During that meeting, I managed to bug their central gathering room, and I had grown very familiar with the vulture men over the past four months.

It was the bug that let me know things were about to change.

Chapter Two

A Day in the Life

I woke to the buzz of my internal alarm clock. I turned it off and languished under the light sheet draped over me for a few more minutes. Summer was in full swing, and even in the depths of the stronghold, the air was warm. I got out of bed and stretched in earnest, bringing my heart rate up and pumping some life through my sleepy limbs. The spiderwebbed mirror leaning against the corner of my shadowy private room reflected several images back at me: a muscular but otherwise unremarkable-looking man just over six feet tall with dark skin, hair, and eyes. I had become leaner during my stay beneath the shattered moon, but that was to be expected. There was no way to pump up my diet like I used to and no gyms, so my muscles diminished to a naturally sustainable size. I developed a strong, wiry form, not unlike the warrior's body in Grecian statues or Roman murals.

I always found it more difficult to sleep during this time of year. I slept best cocooned under a heavy blanket, but the weather only allowed that for five or six months in this climate, so I was chronically under-slept during the summer. Coupled with long-lit days, I got a lot done, and sentients turned a blind eye to the occasional late afternoon nap during the heat of the day.

I went to the kitchen for breakfast and was served soup. Gormond, our cook, had a love affair with soup—soup for breakfast, lunch, and dinner! Soup was an easy way to feed a community and stretch resources, but it was also one of the best ways to ingest liquid in this post-hygienic world. Boiled water was the only clean water, and in some parts, you had to worry about toxic contaminates and radiation. Luckily, Deeplac was not one of those places.

I had done a lot of work on Deeplac's sanitation since my arrival, setting up the exterior relief areas, teaching where—and where not—to deposit bodily waste, and reinforcing basic principles of waste processing to prevent water-borne illnesses. Gormond's passion for soup played its part, even if that entailed eating the same soup for days on end during the depths of winter. Today's soup was pretty good. The flush of spring had passed and we were solidly into summer, providing a wider diversity of ingredients. Unsurprisingly, the soups of autumn, which sometimes bordered on stews, were the best.

As I was eating, Rowan, the traveling worm guy, sat down next to me with his own bowl of soup. Rowan was an invertebrate sentient that traveled from community to community with a pack of earthworms used to aerate soil. I estimated Rowan at eight to nine feet long, although he rarely straightened himself to full height-slash-length as he found curling and bending more natural. His face was like the tip of a giant earthworm; his mouth a hole at the end, and his eyes two dark membranes covered by vertical eyelids. He had eight thin worm-like arms and a matching set of eight legs. His moist skin was sensitive to sunlight, and I never saw Rowan without his tam o'shanter and overcoat. Of all the non-near-human sentients I had seen so far, he was the strangest looking, even more so than the plants. Lovecraft could have created an Elder God from beyond the stars out of him.

"Hey Stonewall! How you doing?" he asked. He had no teeth, so everything he said had a whistle-like quality. It sounded like he was trying to speak and play flute at the same time.

"Doing well. I see you're back for the month," I replied.

"Yep, gotta do my worm dance and get my pay," he responded with what I assumed was a smile. I nodded and kept eating.

Hailed from similar stock, Rowan had the ability to control his worms, giving them basic commands to direct them from field to field. Additionally, his worms moved amazingly fast… for worms, that is. He could charm his worms into moving twenty to thirty times their normal speed after he hit them with his mojo, and they kept that pace for several days. The benefits amplified as his worms passed along their augmentation to any native worms they contacted. I did a back-of-the-envelope calculation the first time I met him, and I figured a monthly visit from him effectively doubled the benefit of typical earthworm soil aeration.

Admittedly, I had too much time on my hands when I first got here, but I was a bit adrift. It was the first time I was up without a mission and in a strange new world, to boot. Botanical math seemed engaging at the time.

"Hey, I heard through the grapevine that you actually captured a rat man and turned him in to the vulture men as tribute, eh?"

"Does that sound like something I'd do?" I immediately deflected. I was surprised, as that information wasn't public knowledge.

"Everyone says you're the tricky sort."

"Well, that's just idle gossip. I'm a straight shooter. If I've got a problem, I solve it directly. Trading rat men to vulture men…who'd have thought?" I responded, hoping to shut down this line of conversation.

"That's what I suspected," Rowan replied with a shrug. "I hear a lot of things traveling around and I'm sure most of them are just stories, but I saw you here and I thought I should ask anyhow."

I finished my soup, said my goodbyes, and headed up to find Abigail, our illustrious leader. She was an early riser and ran a tight ship. She was always on the go, typically with an entourage of sentients, and the fastest way to find her was to go up to the stronghold roof and look around. The sun was already shining down strongly, foretelling of a hot day, and I spotted her in the outer courtyard, talking with Arthur, our armadillian construction foreman.

I beat feet down to the outer courtyard. "Hate to interrupt, but I've something important to ask," I said when I arrived.

Abigail raised an eyebrow, waiting, while Arthur looked a bit put out.

"Did you tell anyone about what went down with the vulture men?"

"Really, Stonewall? Do I look like someone who can't keep a secret?" she responded dismissively. "You've been here, what, a year and a half? You don't even know my last name, do you?" she added for emphasis.

"Point taken. It's just that Rowan said he heard about it through the grapevine, so I wondered if we'd slipped somehow during the drunken celebration after recovering Marilyn, and word got around."

That got their attention.

"I haven't said anything about it," Arthur responded to the unasked question, "and I don't think anyone else has."

"Could someone have seen me do it?"

Abigail and Arthur looked at each other.

"Possibly," she said. "It's unlikely, but it's always possible."

I got the feeling they knew something I didn't, and that they also didn't want to explain it to me right now, so I let it drop. "Okay, just wanted to let you know the word got out somehow."

"Thanks for keeping us informed," Abigail responded.

I looked to the north end of the outer courtyard where all the refugee buildings were being thrown up. "How's it coming along?"

"We're keeping up with the inflow, but if it doesn't slow down, we could get into trouble," Arthur spoke with concern. "So far, we've added about a hundred new temporary residents and we're getting a handful or so new sentients every day."

"Any new information on the barbarian force that's pushing them out?"

"Nope. So far, everyone's encountered a force not dissimilar to the one that attacked us," Abigail affirmed.

"All right. I'm going to check the new arrivals then." I pivoted toward the temporary intake barracks.

About four months ago, Deeplac was attacked twice in a single week. We managed to drive the attackers away with the help of the vulture men, and since then, they'd turned to the north, hitting the Oshkoshers. Their tactics were simple: isolate a community by attacking from the north, which effectively prevented any refugees from retreating toward Oshkosh. But the survivors had to go somewhere, and many of them ended up in Deeplac, the first free settlement south of Oshkosh's domain.

Oshkosh, formally known as the Timocracy of Oshkosh,

established land ownership as the prerequisite for citizenship. Those who did not own land were second-class citizens with no say in the government. They were also typically relegated to backbreaking labor or military service with the promise of land ownership at the end of their term; not that much unlike the promises Rome made to her legionaries so long ago. Inevitably, sentients tired of hard work with promises of delayed rewards—especially if they never came to fruition—and there was always a trickle of sentients leaving Oshkosh, seeking better fortunes in the free settlements to the south. However, with the recent invasions, the trickle was quickly turning into a stream, with worries of becoming a deluge.

Every morning, I checked on the new arrivals from the prior day to give them a health inspection. While useful, my medical background had its limits; I was never trained on the anatomy and physiology of anything but pure humans, and my botany PhD allowed some extrapolation to the plant-based sentients, but most of the time I was simply making educated guesses; better than pure conjecture, but not by much.

The influx of refugees also meant a rise in the number of sentients in Deeplac, as many decided to stay with us and become part of our community. Over the past four months, we've doubled in population. Unlike Oshkosh, everyone in Deeplac had a say in important decisions that affected the community, with the elder council retaining overriding abilities, Abigail, being the leader of said council. Unbeknownst to most, Abigail was a mind reader, but to the majority of Deeplac's sentients, she merely appeared a prudent leader who was a good judge of character and decisive in a jam. She picked the members of the elder council, ensuring different points of view all working toward congruent goals.

Deeplac had an open-door policy and accepted any sentient that brought a useful skill with them, and Abigail's abilities made it easy to pick out the bad eggs or any infiltrators among the evacuees. Regretfully, there were a lot of bad eggs beneath the shattered moon, and we escorted them out of our gates the instant she detected untoward intentions. Everyone in Deeplac went through the same process—my mycological ability convinced them to let me stay. Everyone loves a good mushroom.

As you can see, everything relied upon Abigail, even though she would say otherwise. She appeared to be a completely normal human in her early 60s, with salt-and-pepper hair. She was fit and trim for her age with an autocratic demeanor—she knew what was best and that was enough discussion. Normally that'd annoy me, but she was both smart and wise, correct in her judgment far more than incorrect. It's true that mind reading gave her better information on which to base her decisions, but if she were a fool, it wouldn't save her from making poor choices.

I arrived at the intake barracks and found a single sentient waiting for me. She was of an animal origin that I couldn't place, perhaps guinea pig, but regardless, she was as healthy as an ox and overwhelmingly grateful to be here. I led her into the main refugee barracks but before I could introduce her, a small band broke into tears and ran up to joyfully greet her. I was glad for the happy reunion, even though it intensified the heartbreak of others in the room who were still afraid that it would never be their missing loved one escorted through the door.

The first of my morning tasks done, I went to check on my mushroom farm, which was located in one of the basements of the stronghold where the temperature was best regulated and light didn't reach. I opened the door to ten large hanging burlap sacks sprouting oyster mushrooms. Grabbing a nearby basket, I picked the mature ones and left the rest for later days. I spent ten minutes cranking the hand fan attached to ducting that ran outside to make sure the air circulated. Mushrooms exhaled carbon monoxide, and you had to take care of it.

While I drove the fan, I reviewed my bug's recording. It captured everything twenty-four hours a day, so I developed a program that screened for certain voices, allowing me to jump to the conversations that included influential vulture men. I also created key words that would immediately flag my attention, like "invade," "assault," and "attack," etc. It wasn't as precise as I would like it to be, but it allowed me to review the material in a few hours each day, opposed to the sixteen or so hours it would take without shortcuts. I could always dig into the minutia if something drew my interest.

Normally, I waited until the evening to sift through the recordings, but the mourning period for the recently deceased William Howard Spence III ended this dawn. The board, locked and unable to choose a successor, was supposed to make an announcement on how to proceed.

Much of the discussion was in their strange avian dialect, which I had yet to decipher. Thankfully, whenever they discussed important business, they used English, presumably because it was the language of the ancient corporation. I jumped to where the intelligible voices started and listened in.

"I would like to welcome all to this open meeting," the Aldrich Yates Whitaker IV started. He was the chairman of the board. His voice was weak, and I imagined him to be an old vulture man, like the recently deceased CEO.

"As you all know, we have taken the official three days' bereavement time to mourn the passing of the William Howard Spence III, and during this period, the board performed its sacred duty of deciding who is to become the next CEO of our great company," he continued as the noises in the background settled down to silence.

"This task has proved most difficult. We have consulted and debated for these past three days, and none of us have changed our deeply held beliefs regarding which among us should take the reins of our ship and guide us to a prosperous future. With the steady hand of our late CEO, we reported solid quarterly and year-over-year earnings, meeting our overall expectations from both a top-line and bottom-line perspective as he drove double-digit gains, leveraging the benefits of our unique brand."

I told you they were nuts. You should be thankful you didn't have to listen to four months of this utter gobbledygook they considered proper speech.

"Because of this, we have decided to run a competition starting the day following tribute day, and continuing for three months. During the next quarter, each of the two claimants to the position of William Howard Spence III shall demonstrate what they can individually provide to our great company. May the best vulture man win, and we look forward to recognizing the best among us as our rightful leader!"

Judging by the massive outcry of hisses, caws, and croaks, the vulture men loved this decision. I, on the other hand, immediately realized the implications for Deeplac. I had to let Abigail know, but that meant coming clean regarding my bug, a deliberate omission on my part up until now, mostly because before I bugged the vulture men, I had bugged her.

She was a reasonable person, but everyone got angry from time to time, and she really wasn't someone you wanted to piss off.

Chapter Three

It Is Better to Ask Forgiveness

I found Abigail along the center of the southern wall, where the raiders had attacked. After consideration, the council decided to expand the area outward to plant an apple orchard. They settled on a triangular design with a new tower at the tip to make that section of the wall more defensible. The southern wall took on the appearance of a Vauban star construction.

I strode up her and waited for her attention.

"I already know."

"What?"

"I already know you bugged me."

I breathed a sigh of relief. "Well, that makes this easier then."

She turned and looked me in the eyes. "You really are a presumptuous asshole, Stonewall."

You just don't like me because we're like two peas in a pod, I thought.

She came in real close and whispered in my ear, "You wish you lived in my pod. We don't get caught in my pod."

She backed off and loudly dressed me down in front of the

others. No one knew what I did, but they knew they didn't want to be near me, lest Abigail's wrath rub off on them. I didn't walk away because, well, because she was right. I was who I was, that was what I did. I was better than I used to be, but still a work in progress. I understood that she needed to properly vent her frustration because she knew that I knew she would always put Deeplac's needs ahead of her own. As long as my value to Deeplac was greater than the annoyance I put her and the council through, she would eventually see things my way.

I would also like to take this moment to remind you that you shouldn't think the above when you're currently being yelled at by a mind reader.

"Go loiter somewhere else, Stonewall. Council chambers after dinner," she dismissed me and returned to the needs of her community.

"You got it," I capitulated and walked away.

Finding myself unoccupied for a few hours, I set off to visit Marilyn and Elissa. I liked to drop by every so often to see what they were working on and if they had come up with any new exceptional items. However, they weren't in their shop that morning; they were on the roof of the stronghold, testing out one of their new creations.

"Hey Stonewall! You gotta come over here and see this!" Elissa yelled at me from across the inner courtyard. It was nice to hear someone excited to see me after the verbal bruising I took. It was hard to brood around Elissa; her excitement and bubbly personality were infectious.

I circled around the massive grates covering the inner courtyard—they would easily hold my weight, but no sense tempting fate—and came just in time to see Elissa pick up two pieces of scrap metal that must have weighed at least two hundred pounds each. She held them with gloved hands and struck a bodybuilder's pose to show off her "guns." She didn't hold the pose for long, because she was laughing too hard at her own joke.

"I assume it's the gloves?" I motioned toward the pair of oversized dark-leather gloves etched with silver circuitry that I had never seen before.

"Well, isn't he the smart one," she said to Marilyn, who was also enjoying her antics.

"I'm also assuming it doesn't actually make you strong and instead does something to the metal?"

Elissa put down the metal and mimed her best faux-shocked face. "Another correct answer. Let's see if you can go three for three," she quipped. "You want to take a stab at how it works?"

"No. No, I do not. I never get three right answers in a row with you two," I declined graciously.

"You're no fun today," she harrumphed as she took off the gloves and handed them to me. I put them on and grabbed the two pieces of scrap metal, lifting them into the air as if they weighed five pounds each.

"Ah," I said with appreciation. "That's a fine bit of work."

Marilyn smiled and explained, "The gloves work on any magnetic metal they encounter, setting up an anti-gravity field around the object while concurrently reading the electrical current in the tendons in your palm, preventing release until you choose to let go. While wearing these gloves, you could never be disarmed against your will, but that is more of an incidental benefit. The real use will come from the increased carrying capacity for scavengers."

I put down the scrap, took off the gloves, and handed them to Marilyn. "I see you made them oversized."

"I wanted to make sure they'd fit the greatest number of sentients. If they're too big, you can always tie them on with some rope."

I tilted my head toward them. "You do realize that you've created a nice weapon, right?"

Both of them looked at me quizzically.

"Imagine if I decided to throw those things at you," I postulated, pointing to the scrap metal.

They both openly laughed, and Marilyn said, "No, no, no, it doesn't work that way. Here try it, but watch your feet." She handed the gloves back to me.

I put them on and tried to throw one of the pieces of scrap in a careful, underhanded throw. The metal immediately dropped like a stone. I couldn't rightly say I "threw" it anywhere.

"The metal still has the same mass, silly!" Elissa taunted.

"The force you're applying to throw it doesn't affect it. You'd have to apply enough force to actually move the metal to throw it, the same as if you weren't wearing the gloves."

Marilyn nodded at her apprentice's excellent explanation. Elissa's ear tuffs flicked with pride.

"Well then," I acquiesced that point to their knowledge, "there still another use you hadn't thought of."

They looked intrigued, so I continued, "If the gloves don't let go of metal until you want them to, you could use them to hang onto a piece of metal, provided the gloves were secured tightly enough around your hands so that they couldn't slip off."

Marilyn's striped tail flicked while she looked up and to the left, the classic image of someone in thought, and then looked straight at me. "I do believe you're right," she said with slight amazement. "Which means you almost went three for three today. You're getting better!" she said, engulfing me in one of her plentiful hugs.

Marilyn's hugs were both comforting and disconcerting to me. They were an extension of her big heart and genuine affection, but such unabashed authenticity was new to me. I understood stoicism, sarcasm, and even cruelty; but up until Deeplac, sincerity elicited suspicion. It took me a long time to get use to her hugs, and even now, I made my escape from her furry arms as soon as I could without offending her, but I hung on a little longer each time. A work in progress.

"I don't think Abigail's contacted you yet, but I'm going to be speaking to the council after dinner tonight," I said to change the subject.

"What's it about?" she asked, now all business.

"I don't really want to say yet, but I thought I should pass along word to you that a meeting is going to happen."

"Gotcha," she said. "See you then?"

"See you then," I said with a head bob, walking away. "I've got to get some things ready for the meeting, so if you or anyone else needs me, I'll be downstairs for the rest of the day."

I took the stairs down to my room and spent the next few hours going back and forth over all the recordings I had of the vulture men that were important to my coming presentation. I needed to make a solid case if I wanted them to come to my way of solving this problem.

After dinner, I went to the council chamber and found the elders were already there. I made my greetings and jumped right to the issue at hand.

"As I'm sure Abigail's informed you, I planted a listening device in the central gathering room of the vulture men's headquarters when I was handing over the rat man I captured. Over the past four months, I have been listening in on their discussions and have important news. Their chief died three days ago and the vulture men haven't been able to select another, so they've decided to have a competition between the two primary contenders. The competition starts next month and is slated to run for the next three months, during which time the contenders will be judged based upon how much wealth they can bring back to their aerie. I suspect that starting next month, each of the claimants is going to ask for tribute."

All of the elders understood what that meant. Only four months ago, Deeplac was teetering on the edge of bankruptcy, as it pays monthly tribute to both the vulture men and to the Oshkoshers. Paying double tribute to just the vulture men for three months wasn't possible this soon after their recovery from the wastelanders' attack. With Marilyn's return, Abigail soldiered through the payments, saving the two tribute favors I'd earned via my rat man trade, but even with this cushion, Deeplac wasn't going to be able to absorb the costs without serious effort.

"As Abigail's asked me to speak freely, I have some ideas on how to alleviate this situation. First and foremost, I think it's time to tell the Oshkoshers to take a hike. Based on what I have picked up from the refugees, they're neck deep in their own pickle right now, and the payment that has been going to them could be used to shore up our defenses against them if they manage to kick out the invading muties and come after us for failure of payment. I may be biased by the bleak view from the survivors, but I'm only giving that scenario a fifty-fifty chance. And if Oshkosh falls to the muties, we would definitely benefit from added defenses, as the muties will eventually come our way again."

I got a few instant nods; they had obviously been discussing our circumstances and some on the council already thought as I did. Abigail, being Abigail, maintained her normal impassive mien.

"If we decide to do that," I continued, "we'd pay the vulture men like normal this month, and then give one tribute token to each of the vying vulture men demanding tribute. We could spin it as 'we don't want to take sides in an internal company matter, so we're trying to treat each applicant as equally as possible.' I think they'd buy that and may even find it admirable, given their attachment to ancient corporate speak.

"This would mean only paying one tribute over the next two months instead of four tributes. That's a lot of resources we can divert into buying the one thing we need for independence from the vulture men: rifles. Our main weakness against them is our lack of firearms that can reliably target them as they're flying overhead. If we could pick off just a couple every time they attack, they'll eventually leave us alone.

"But better than having excess trade goods for rifles, which are almost impossible to trade for right now with the muties banging up Oshkosh, I think I know where I may be able to scavenge some."

That got their full and undivided attention.

"I'm going to come clean to the council about an ability I have that I haven't told anyone about." I looked at Abigail. "Which I think I've even successfully hidden from you. I have a full set of maps in my head."

Abigail's stone face cracked with surprise. She hadn't known. At least I had managed to keep some secrets.

"I'm augmented with a computer that has massive amounts of information stored on it. This means I have full maps from my time, down to addresses and names of business. According to my maps there are, or I should say, as of 2112, there were thirteen different gun shops within a fifteen-mile radius of Deeplac. Some of these places may have avoided the strange ruin regeneration effect, and there's a decent chance that we can find one unlooted shop. Syncing up my map and your map, I can indicate where to scavenge for the best chances. And more importantly, I can show you where to dig."

Puzzled eyebrows raised around the room at the suggestion of digging for scavenge.

"I think the best chance of finding a cache of weapons isn't going to be in a ruin, it's going to be in one of the massive piles of rubble. Rubble doesn't regenerate like ruins do, and because of that, everyone assumes the rubble has already been picked clean over the generations. I'm assuming otherwise. I'm assuming the good stuff we're looking for is still out there, buried where no one even bothers to look.

"I've seen your detailed map of this area. I've memorized it. There are twelve locations in the rubble that used to be gun shops. I propose we start digging in those locations and hope one of them pans out."

I folded my hands in front of me, indicating an end to my proposal. I had given them a lot to think about in a short time, and I waited in silence for a response. Looking around the table, each of them were doing their own internal math. It was a tense twenty seconds before anyone spoke.

"If we go down this road, we're committed," Arthur addressed the table. He was the most conservative of the elders.

"That's the truth," Morien agreed. "If we do this, we're going to have two enemies at the end of the day, regardless if one of them is the Oshkoshers or the mutie army that's attacking them."

"What's the alternative?" Grendel asked. "We spend our days struggling to meet the demands of one group that provides us no help, and another group that only provides help at great cost? We've doubled in size in these past four months, and that's stretching us very thin."

"The vulture men in particular ensure that they're always taking just enough to keep us dependent upon them," I interjected an observation that seemed obvious to me, but I couldn't be sure they saw it, too, as tribute to the vulture men was always the way it had been done. "Note how they always confiscate all of the guns as tribute after an attack whenever they help us. They know their vulnerability, and do their best to make sure we don't discover it or have the strength to fight back."

Marilyn concurred, adding, "They're always demanding

weapons as tribute as well."

Will the immigrants give us problems if Oshkosh survives and comes knocking at our door? Broagh broadcast while looking at Abigail.

She shook her head. "From what I can read, most of them are very grateful to be here, and many of them express regret that they waited so long to change allegiances. About half to three-quarters of them weren't landowners, so they have nothing to return to except servitude. I don't think we'll have any internal problems, but I'll keep my eye on it, of course."

"Is there a way for us to hedge our bets—a way for us to focus on one group without taking on the other?" Arthur asked.

No one at the table answered, so I ventured, "If we act quickly and decisively, we may not have to face them at the same time. If we find enough weapons to repel the vulture men, we'll be free of them before we face a possible Oshkosh retaliation. Oshkosh has to beat back the wasteland raiders before they can get to us, and based on where the refugees are coming from, the invaders still have a ways to go before they reach the heart of Oshkosh. We have a window of opportunity that I think we should grab, because I don't know if it will open again."

Everyone looked down pensively, and eventually Abigail said, "Your idea sounds good to me. I say we go for it."

I was pleasantly surprised she put her support behind

the idea so quickly, but I ran with it and addressed the whole council. "That's great! If you pull out the big detailed map, I'll show you the locations where we could dig and you can decide where to start. I may know the map and the locations of the old gun shops, but I don't really know the terrain, and your local knowledge will be invaluable."

The rest of the meeting went fairly quickly after that. Over the map, I flagged locations and we debated each of their merits and dangers. Eventually, the council established the order of digs over the next two months, but even a quick organizational meeting took a lot of time, and it was nearly dark outside by the time we finished. I headed to my chamber and called it a night.

Chapter Four

Once Bitten, Twice Shy

The next morning dawned with greater purpose than the prior, as I was supposed to meet with Arthur and his digging crew in the outer courtyard in an hour. I rose, stretched, and ate as quickly as I could. I flew through my morning tasks—there were no new immigrants awaiting medical clearance, and I hastily tended my mushrooms while checking the bug for recent chatter. Everything in the past day was in their vulture-man language, so nothing to be gained there.

One of Agent Six's guises was a linguist, and observing language use beneath the shattered moon became one of the ways I passed the time. I had taken to calling the vulture men's speech "Avian V," a linguist's joke of sorts, but it was rather presumptuous to assume all vulture men shared a common tongue, considering I'd only encountered the one group. It was quite possible a different group would have a different language or even no special language at all. Considering all the different languages and dialects humans spoke before the apocalypse, it was a miracle that all the sentients I had encountered so far spoke an intelligible version of English, Spanish, French, or

Finnish rather than a mutie variant or amalgamation.

With all of my long-standing responsibilities met, I joined Arthur in the courtyard along with half of the dozen sentients that made up his construction crew. To my surprise, Broagh was there as well. When the meeting broke yesterday, there was no indication that he would be coming on this mission, but bringing a giant hedgehog wasn't a bad idea on a dig, and I could imagine Abigail wanting another set of elder's eyes on my impetuous butt. Not that I could blame her.

In addition to the digging crew came five guards: Diana, the Blade Witch; Zew, the mohawked warrior who'd walked out of the wasteland; Blaine, the archer of an enchanted bow; Reginald, the towering crack shot; and Ummagumma, the flying bipedal pig. I was doing double duty, navigating to the dig site and joining the guards so the diggers could focus on digging.

"Heya Diana, where's Grendel?" I asked as I walked up. Grendel was supposed to be leading the guards, and it was hard to miss the eight-foot giant.

Diana shrugged and Broagh responded, *He's not here yet, Stonewall. He told me he might be a bit late.* I had finally gotten used to his calm disembodied voice popping up from two feet behind me; I didn't even flinch this time. It only took me a year and a half.

"Okay," I said, and went over our supplies. We were passing through crocophant territory and brought a goodly supply of torches to affix to the ends of our spears. Crocophants were ambush predators with the body and bulk of an African elephant and the head of a crocodile. Because of their bulk, they favored watering holes. I know what you are thinking: which would be worse, a crocodile that could grab you with a strong prehensile trunk or the death roll of a conventional crocodile the size of an elephant? Well, the answer is—it doesn't matter when you're staring down the business end of a crocophant. Luckily, crocophants hated fire and fled before it, so we always made sure we had twice as many torches as we had sentients when traveling near its domain. We only had one crocophant near us, but one was more than enough.

Along with the torches and spears, we had a mix of hammers and shovels as well as a variety of pry bars, the heaviest weighing more than fifty pounds, specially crafted for Grendel by John Smith, Deeplac's resident blacksmith. We also had four wheelbarrows and various sacks, ropes, and pulleys atop a flexible sled pulled by four of the diggers. We were over-packed, but we weren't sure what we'd find in the rubble; no one ever went in as far as we were going. Our destination was past legitimate ruins and a full mile within a massive rubble pile, and no one ever went more than a few dozen yards into rubble zones if they could avoid it.

Grendel and the rest of the diggers arrived shortly after I finished my inspection, and we exited the gates and headed south. We had roughly six miles to go before we entered crocophant territory, and two more after that to get to the dig location.

Diana and Umma took point. Every half hour, Umma took a short flight to get a pig's-eye view of the surrounding area, reducing the chance that we would be surprised by dangerous fauna or an opposing force. I hung out in the back along with Zew, Blaine, and Reginald.

It was a sunny, breezy day, and soon we were sweating as we hiked through the waist-high grass. In smaller groups, it was better to attempt stealth by sticking to the tree line, even if that meant a more roundabout path to your destination. However, there was little point in attempting covert movement with a troop this large carrying as much equipment as we had, so we walked freely. It was a nice change of pace to enjoy the sun and wind without constantly worrying about detection.

Those of us not pulling the sled or carrying a missile weapon wielded spears. Spears were incredibly versatile weapons, and they were the most common armament beneath the shattered moon, since they were easily made given the availability of scavenged rebar. In the hands of a competent warrior, spears were more effective than swords or maces due to their reach, the power of leverage, and their ability to be easily used in groups. There was a reason that spears ruled the battlefields of history until the invention of the gun. But the gun didn't end the spear; armies just affixed bayonets to their guns and went about their business with modern spears. Oh, and let's not forget that you could throw a spear if you weighted them properly, as ours were.

In my prior life as Agent Six, I had little reason to learn how to properly use spears, but I had a change of heart after crawling out of my cryopod and into this world. I had been taking lessons from the more experienced and now considered myself "competent" with the weapon. I had just gotten good enough that Zew agreed to take me on as a private student starting next month. He was the best with the weapon at Deeplac, although Diana was a close second.

Once we were within a mile of known crocophant territory, we broke out the torches and affixed them to the end of our spears via the holders John custom-created for just such a purpose. We kept the torches lit at all times; as an ambush predator, the crocophant had a remarkable ability to remain unseen, especially given its size. None of us ever went to the lake it frequented. It was entirely too dangerous to go anywhere near its chosen water; the damn thing was fast enough to simply run you down if it happened to have a bee up its butt. We had just lit the torches when Umma landed from his latest scouting mission.

"I saw the crocophant! It's about four hundred yards west of here, lounging in its lake," the winded pigman reported.

"Did it seem aware of us?" Grendel asked.

"Not that I could tell," Umma huffed, "but give me a minute to catch my breath and I'll go back up and double check."

"Keep us informed," Grendel replied.

We walked for a few more hundred feet and Umma took to the skies once more, this time flying toward the west as opposed to circling overhead. He was a few hundred yards out when he came barreling back, flying as fast as his little wings could carry him. "It's coming!" he yelled as he landed roughly on the eastern side of our group.

"Spears ready! Missiles fire at will!" Grendel ordered, starting to spin his massive sling.

The crocophant crested the hill between us and its lake, about two hundred yards away. It seemed indifferent to our torches and kept advancing. At one hundred yards, it broke into a charge, and a spurt of mixed missiles flew out from behind our row of spears. They didn't slow it down. Perhaps the creature's thick skin deflected them? The second launch that quickly followed met with a similar lack of effect.

Blaine, use your fiery arrows, Broagh broadcast over the whirl of slings. *It should flee before them!*

Blaine obliged and the next salvo featured one of her bow's magical arrows. Coated with magical fire, the arrow burrowed completely through the crocophant as if it weren't there, going in one side of its head and coming out the opposite side of its rear.

What the...? I thought and then realized the danger—the grass wasn't parting as the crocophant charged.

"It's not really there! It's an illusion! Everyone circle up with spears out now!" I yelled, but I was too late.

The image before us flickered and disappeared, replaced by a terrifying reptilian roar behind our spear line—an angry bellow mixed with surprising pain. I turned, dropping my spear and drawing my blaster, only to see the horrible looming mass of the beast directly upon us, Broagh already in its toothy maw. The crocodilian face looked befuddled when it got a pincushion instead of a tasty treat and quickly spat out the giant hedgehog, long quills sticking out of its maw. The elephantine mass wheeled around and fled the scene, peppered with Blaine's fiery arrows and Umma's crossbow from the air.

"Broagh?" Grendel yelled.

I'm fine, he broadcast to us all as he popped up out of the tall grass.

What ill luck caused the crocophant to attack the lone member of our crew that was literally covered in spines, I'll never know. But the sight of eight tons of killing machine spitting out a giant hedgehog and running away in pain and confusion while being pursued by a flying pig wielding a crossbow will remain with me for the rest of my life.

Knowing that Broagh was uninjured settled our nerves. Then the laughter began. You take your humor where you can get it beneath the shattered moon.

Chapter Five

There's Guns in Them Thar Hills

We regained our composure and regrouped, now traveling in a circular mob, spears out. Umma resumed his periodic aerial scouting and I moved up to the front of the pack where Grendel and Broagh were.

"What just happened?" I asked. "I was under the impression that the crocophant couldn't do anything special. They're just big, dumb, and hungry."

Grendel shot me an annoyed look. "Up until now, the crocophant had displayed no extraordinary abilities. We've been coming this way for years, so it's unlikely that we wouldn't have seen it use the ability before."

Which means it's developed the ability since our last encounter, roughly three months ago, Broagh added.

"Which suggests that it encountered some sort of mutagen, and consequently, we could encounter some sort of mutagen," Grendel emphasized.

"Mutagen?"

"Stuff that changes you," he explained.

"I know what it means," I retorted. "I just wanted to know

if it was something we need to worry about. Is it typical to have mutagens lying around?"

Not around here, no, Broagh answered. *Mutagens are most prevalent in the massive ancient ruins, and less common in the wastelands. Prior to the crocophant developing a new ability, we didn't think there was anything mutagenic in this area.*

"Does this stuff have a particular look to it?"

The most common of the mutagens is the glowing green goo. It's not dangerous if you don't touch it, and most sentients are naturally smart enough to avoid touching gloop that glows to begin with. Animals, on the other hand...

"Alrighty then, I'll make sure not to touch anything that glows green."

"Good for you," Grendel said. "Now go back and guard the rear; we were having a conversation before you interrupted." He dismissed me. *Someone's touchy today,* I thought as I dropped back to the rear and took up my position between Blaine and Zew.

We forged ahead in silence; the small hillocks of grass-covered dirt transitioned into vestiges of suburban structures. We naturally tightened our formation into a short column as the grass gave way to an ancient road and the hillocks to husks of ravaged buildings. Ahead of us loomed larger constructions, some as tall as eight or ten stories, their darkened interiors creating squares of shadow in an otherwise bright day.

Back in the 2100s, I had cause to travel through many

abandoned areas. I was most familiar with Plymouth, Montserrat and Pripyat, Ukraine, having spent a lot of training time there for The Company. Neither approached the scale of the ruins beneath the shattered moon, and I'd only been in the smaller ones. I could only imagine what places like Chicago or New York must be like now—tens of miles of endless decay.

As we entered full-blown urban blight, Umma continued his reconnaissance flights, landing on the rooftops to constantly maintain an elevated position as we progressed deeper into the ancients' realm. Like others under the shattered moon, these ruins didn't make sense. Some structures look recently abandoned while others were skeletonized and decrepit, both types meeting incongruent architecture from various times. Labeled "highly regenerative" on Deeplac's map, this area changed more rapidly, heightening our sensitivity to shifts in our immediate environs.

We'd gone about half a mile into the ruin when Broagh broadcast, *Everyone stop, I'm detecting nearby sentients.*

We halted, weapons ready, and Grendel announced, "We know you're there; you might as well come out!"

A group of five sentients emanated from the shadows, all clothed in tight gray suits that reminded me of what ninjas wore in the movies from my time. We all breathed a sigh of relief; they were members of the Church of Parkour. The Church was one of the few nationwide organizations operating after the apocalypse, and thankfully, friendly to Deeplac and the other settlements beneath the shattered moon. As the name implies, they believed that proper bodily movement is the path that liberates the spirit from the wheel of reincarnation. They were consummate ruin-runners, and were beneficial forces in the communities that hosted one of their cells, or septs, as they called them. I've met members of the Church twice before—the first was in Deeplac when they were trading rolled steel for grain, and the second was in the ruins southeast of Deeplac on a scavenging run. They're some of the nicest sentients to meet, if a little formal.

"Greetings, fellow cousins of the stride, we mean you no harm and were pausing only to allow you passage before continuing our meditations," the leader of the group declared.

"As we to you," Grendel replied solemnly.

"I am Hrilarth, master of this sept. We have no new information to share about our path. All is as it has been." It was their ritualistic way of informing us that they hadn't seen anything unusual on their trip.

"I am Grendel, leader of this band from Deeplac," our colossal speaker replied in kind. "We have new information: the crocophant that roams this land has mutated and now casts illusions, misleading viewers into believing it approaches from one direction while it actually approaches from the opposite."

"Truly that is useful information, cousin," Hrilarth responded. "You do the Church a great service and we thank you." All of the members of the sept bowed deeply.

"It is my pleasure to serve the Church. Now we must be on our way. Good pathing."

"And good pathing to you!"

We continued on our way and the Church of Parkour's members faded back into the shadows. I tried to keep my eyes on them but failed. I wonder how many other times they've been around and I never noticed.

"Zew, do they always disappear like that?" I quietly asked my nearby companion.

"Yep. They've got a knack for it," he replied, equally quiet. "They can also run like hell, nothing seems to really slow them down. They don't fight much, so don't count on them to have your back unless they owe you something."

A hush fell over us as we moved past the regenerative ruins into the ravaged rubble. Unable to maintain formation, we settled into a single-person column and made our way deeper into the zone that no one ever visits. Grendel put me in the front, as I was the only one who could tell when we'd arrived at our destination. My computer keeps track of the distance and direction of my travels using a biofeedback measuring stick; basically, it knows how long each of my steps are and calculates distance for me. It was useful as Agent Six, and incredibly useful now in a post-GPS world. It meant that I could lead the group right to the front door of the gun shop, as long as my internal map was congruent with my boots on the ground.

The farther we advanced, the quieter it grew. The familiar

call of birds diminished, and soon the scuffling, clanking, and heavy breathing of the sentients behind me was the only ambient noise. Although I heard no sounds of life in the rubble, the dusty ground betrayed its existence. Littered throughout the path were insect and reptile trails, along with the rarer large imprint of a wild dog, cat, or unihorn jackal. None concerned me except a single mark made by a large cat, roughly the size of a lion. Whatever made that mark could be dangerous, but shouldn't be an issue for a group as large as ours.

After a rough hour of hauling our gear through the debris, we arrived at the location. We took a moment to catch our breath and slake our thirst before diving into the rubble. The sleds were unpacked, and sentients teamed up in trios: one with a pry bar, a second with a shovel, and the third to move the earth away from the dig site. Every twenty minutes or so, they'd change places, allowing each of the sentients relative rest when their time to haul dirt came around.

When we reviewed potential targets, Shrenk's Gunsmithing was at the top of the list, a gun shop that had been in business since 1911, according to my records. That was the longest window of operation of any of the potential dig sites, giving us the best chance it was still operating on whatever date the apocalypse happened. Which I didn't know. Which no one knew.

Bear with me—this has been bothering me ever since I got here. If the apocalypse happened sometime not much later than

2112, which is where my records end, none of the amazing future tech like the silver egg could exist. But if it happened far enough in the future for the revolutionary tech to be built, the ruins should look far different from what I have in my head in terms of map correlation and architectural styles. Based on how close my internal map of Gurnee Mills Mall in 2112 was to the rat men's lair of the post-apocalypse, and the fact that ninety-five percent or more of the ruins look familiar to me, indicates that the apocalypse had to have happened fairly soon after 2112.

Additionally, if the apocalypse happened so far in the future as the advanced tech and five percent of the ruins suggest, there's no way so many old things would still be around. For example, why are there so many firearms from the twentieth century, when they would all be collector's items if the apocalypse happened in 2200 or beyond? None of it makes any sense. The physical evidence of the ancients is a hodgepodge of different ages smashed together, and the world is a tangled knot of various times. Which is why we decided on Shrenk's; if the world is a knot of timelines, the best string to pull is the longest one.

Grendel called for lunch after two hours of digging, and we tucked into our food, refreshing ourselves with water and a single shot of whiskey. Breaking out the whiskey was a nice touch. The shadows retreated as the sun rose higher in the sky, bringing more warmth to us all. It was back to work and less than an hour later, we hit pay dirt.

"Oi! I've found something!" one of the diggers hollered.

I left my guard post and looked down into the hole. Sure enough, she broke through the surface, revealing a cavity beneath.

"We need some light! Bring a flashlight!" I yelled. Reginald, the closest guard to the pack train, grabbed a flashlight and brought it to me, pushing past the others who circled the black ring that opened beneath us.

I tied a rope around my ankle and handed it to Reginald as he handed me the flashlight. "Just in case you need to pull me out," I said, and then slid down the side of the hole, poking my light and head through the surface and into the void.

"It's a basement!" I yelled to the waiting crowd. Although one side was partially collapsed, an empty niche led off to the south beyond my light's purview. "I'm going to see if I can crawl in!" I announced and then slid through the hole, falling four feet before catching myself in a one-armed handstand. I righted myself and popped my head out of the hole. "I'm going to undo the rope and scout for a minute. I'll be right back." I threw the rope out and ducked down to explore.

I crawled south for a few yards, squeezing through a tight spot before the earth opened before me, displaying a relatively intact basement. I clambered into the buried room, again managing a one-armed handstand before coming to my feet.

A dozen wood and glass cases surrounded me, bearing

rack after rack of long arms—shotguns and rifles of all types. Carefully pulling open the cabinets beneath the display cases, I found box after box of ammunition; enough to free Deeplac from both the Oshkoshers and the vulture men, if they came looking for a fight.

I crawled back to the hole and pushed myself out to the dust-stained and expectant faces of the diggers. "I've got good news and bad news; the good news is that we've found what we're looking for"—cheers rang out at my announcement and I had to raise my voice—"and the bad news is…" I paused for dramatic effect, "you lot are going to have sore backs hauling all the loot home!"

Emptying the basement of its treasure took the better part of an hour. In total, there were forty-two rifles, thirty-eight shotguns, forty-four pistols, and six thousand rounds of ammunition divided amongst the various weapons. In addition, there were fifty rifle scopes, twelve pistol scopes, five laser sights—one for a rifle—and a raft of non-lethal defenses such as pepper spray and stun guns, most of which still had charge.

The usual rules of scavenging were overridden in the case of a massive find like this. Under these circumstances, Deeplac would get half, and those of us who found the items would split the remainder. Each of the diggers was going to walk away with at least a firearm and ammunition. That fact put smiles on dusty, sweat-river faces; the sun was blazing relentlessly, baking the dirt on the surface at close to 95°F. No matter how stuffy it got down here in the basement, at least it was cool.

I'd almost finished cleaning out the place when I noticed the bottom edge of an old safe buried in the floor. I whipped out my plasma cutter and worked away a hole large enough for my arm. I then cut through the corner of the safe, taking care to avoid damaging whatever was inside. I stuck my hand through and felt three boxes. After widening the hole by a few more inches, I fished out the first box—sixty mint gold American Eagles inside.

The second box was heavy, military green, and contained something that shouldn't have been in a private gun shop—two hundred-foot spools of flexible linear shaped charge, marked as twenty grains per foot. The two spools weighed about thirty pounds each. There weren't any detonators, but there was still one more box in the safe.

The third box contained stacks of now-worthless hundred dollar bills along with a smaller box containing six timed detonators as well a radio-control switch.

Well, well, well…. There's a lot that could be done even with the minimal amount of explosives I'd found, especially in the hands of an expert. It was nice to have those options back in my arsenal. I was pretty sure no one was going to pick the explosives over a firearm or more gold, so this box was going to be mine.

I emerged carrying the three boxes and as expected, the

announcement of a trove of gold coins unleashed another round of snaggletoothed smiles from those waiting on the hot surface. None had expected such a great return for a day's labor, and there would be celebrations tonight. I pulled myself up from the dig and handed everything off to Grendel, who catalogued the items and placed them on the sleds. Once back in Deeplac, we would divide everything amongst the crew, but Arthur, Grendel and Broagh thought it wise to distribute rifles to each crewmember; there's no reason to have rifles on a sled while you're carrying spears for weapons.

We left for home victorious and cheerful, cycling through a bunch of marching songs. Normally Grendel, or Broagh would have put the kibosh on such antics, but they knew more than the rest what the find meant for Deeplac, and they both heartily sang along. I even heard Arthur hum along. There are times when you are so full of life that when you stare out to face the world, you sense it flinch back, shying away from your challenge. I find it best to enjoy these moments when you can, because they don't last for long—confidence evolves into hubris, and then you are just tempting fate.

The songs and frivolity died off once we returned to the ruins. The shattered remnants of a mighty civilization sapped our glee as the massive gray gravestones of a world long-gone tapped us on the shoulder, reminding us that fate is patient, never forgets, and has taken down life after life, age after age.

We lit and fixed torches to spears, circled up, and set a brisk pace across crocophant territory. With so much loot on the sled, Grendel relieved the four-man sled team and pulled the sled himself. Now that we all had rifles, they were better used as guards than pack animals anyway. We picked up the pace, eager to get back and celebrate. Umma reported a group of a dozen sentients traveling south a few miles to the west of us. Grendel had him keep an eye on them, but they kept on their same bearing.

We dispersed a large pack of bunnysharks that took down a throttle horse, a vile carnivorous horse-like creature with tentacles on their heads where their mouths should be. They typically traveled in small herds, and with a flick of its head, a throttle horse launched a tentacle that would strange you if it hit your neck. Needless to say, I kept my distance when I saw them on the move, but curiosity got the better of me and I poked at what remained of the carcass.

When the wall of Deeplac finally came into view in the early evening, Umma flew off to find Abigail so she could meet us at the gates. She stood at the front as we arrived five minutes later.

"A complete success!" Grendel shouted out while we were still a good hundred yards away.

I swear to God that Abigail actually leapt with excitement, mimicking Elissa's trademark sign of joy.

As soon as we'd pulled everything into the outer courtyard and closed the gates, she went to inspect the rest of the haul, already eyeing the new rifles the crew sported. As she worked her way through the list with Grendel, other sentients of Deeplac heard the news and soon most of the village surrounded us.

The joyful mood was contagious, and once the whiskey made its appearance, we had a full-blown festival on our hands.

Chapter Six

Vulture Capitalism

Stonewall, wake up. Abigail wants to talk to you, Broagh broadcast loud enough to wake me from a hard sleep. I opened my heavy eyes and looked around; he was standing in the doorway of my chamber.

"All right. Give me five minutes. Where is she?"

Southern wall near the new construction.

"Make it ten minutes, then. Any idea what she wants?"

Nope, he said, dropping the curtain as he left.

I sighed and got dressed. Even though I'd gotten all buddy-buddy with the members of the elder council over the past season, I'd rather not get a summons early in the morning. In my experience, they are rarely to deliver good news.

The sky was cloudy today, a delightful break from the relentless sun and heat of the typical summer day. It was temperate enough that I wasn't even sweating when I found Abigail outside. I nodded at her when I arrived and waited a distance away until she was ready to talk to me.

"Stonewall, thanks for showing up so quickly," she started. I'd like to interpret her tone to mean she'd softened on me, but

I'm smarter than that. It took more than a successful mission or two to do that.

"No problem. What's up?"

"How many rubble-raiding operations do you think you could pull off before our next tribute to the vulture men ten days from now?"

"Give me a minute for some calculations, would you?"

She waved her hand at me to proceed and returned to the orchard. Herbert, the sentient kudzu who enriches the soil by tasting it, had started the apple trees a year ago in large clay pots and was in the process of planting them. They wouldn't bear fruit for at least five years, but once they did, they could start juicing them for hard cider, a trade good in high demand.

After running the numbers, I approached her. "I think we could reliably do four runs, five if we push it. In this heat, each run really takes it out of the crew and I wouldn't want to do more than one every other day. I'd favor four over five; it gives us two days wiggle room."

She nodded and I continued, "We could do more runs, perhaps up to seven or eight if you expanded beyond just using the digging crew. The big find yesterday will entice those who missed out to get their chance. If you opened it up, perhaps by some sort of lottery, we could excavate more sites and make more sentients happy in the process."

"That's not a bad idea. Do you think you could plan and lead seven expeditions in the next ten days?"

"Yeah, it'll be tiring, but I can do it. I'd rotate through the elder council members, though. No need to have all three of them on each dig; I'd go back and forth between Arthur and Broagh, as they're both great diggers."

"Let's do that then. Could you plot out the seven expeditions you think have the greatest chance of success within our new window, and inform the council of the plan after dinner?"

"Can do," I assented. I blame Abigail and her polite compliments—they threw me off balance and I'd committed myself to a rough ten days. I left her to her work before I could get roped into more work, and finished my daily routine before holing up in my chamber to plan my presentation. Luckily, my other obligations didn't weigh heavy upon my time.

The meeting went smoothly, and the council approved each of my suggestions. Afterward, they announced a lottery system wherein the digging crew would be randomly selected from a group of sentients who put themselves in the running. Everyone seemed to like the idea, although there was a bit of grumbling from Arthur's normal digging crew; you can't please everyone all the time.

After the drawing, I packed myself into bed and reviewed the day's vulture-man recording before going to sleep. Nothing of particular note; I wish I'd been able to plant a couple of bugs throughout the building, but I had only the one. Since the room I bugged was the main gathering space for the vulture men, I don't get any of the really good gossip—the conversations tend to be casual or overtly public. The location's good for learning the large events—public speeches, meetings, et cetera—but that's it.

The next nine days were a blur of activity. In total, we made eight runs into the rubble, none of which sent us through dangerous territory like the first, and the size of our group dissuaded the more casual dangers. Only the last of the digs panned out. The weapons in the last dig were in worse shape than the first, because we had to extract them from the earth like dinosaur bones, apropos as "modern" firearms were relics of a past age that required careful excavation. We returned with a dozen operable long arms, an equal number of pistols, and a little more than a thousand rounds of ammunition in various calibers. Additionally, we brought back a dozen inoperable firearms that Marilyn and Elissa could work on, so there was a chance that we could get a few more out of the bunch.

Two out of nine didn't seem like a great track record, but the council was thrilled with the results. We'd found a new way of extracting resources that other communities couldn't capitalize on because they didn't have the precise maps I did. They quickly extrapolated that ratio out to the possible digs we could do, and for once, I had to rein in their enthusiasm and caution not to expect such a return. That said, even if we only did half as well and got one good hit per month of digging, it was quite a windfall for a community that was used to paying tribute to two groups.

Tribute collection was a monthly affair; paying off both Oshkosh and the vulture men, each in their peculiar way. The Oshkoshers were straightforward—they sent an envoy with a score of guards that arrived in the evening, spent the night, and then moved on the next morning. They came these past three months despite the raiders' attack on their southern border, but they looked progressively harried with each visit.

And then there were the vulture men.

A group of six led by the Linda Jeannette Robickow, HR Director, arrived early in the day, only an hour after sunrise. The vulture men demanded everyone stay inside the stronghold during the transaction, refusing to land unless Deeplac was still, dealing exclusively with the elder council members bearing their tribute. So once a month, the entire population of Deeplac—except the cooks and tribute makers—took the day off. They could sleep in and lounge about, taking a late breakfast. Those who woke early spent the first few hours of the day in cozy community, one that was a bit strained over the past few months since the raiders from the wasteland had started warring with Oshkosh.

The vulture men didn't discriminate between a resident of Deeplac and the recent refugees from the north—all had to be out of sight. Abigail used Elissa's scent-scrubbing spray to clean out Marilyn's old quarters outside of the stronghold for the newest arrivals I hadn't cleared as disease-free, but everyone else went into the stronghold, which Abigail loathed. She didn't want anyone but those who'd sworn an oath to our community knowing the layout of our fortress, but her hands were tied. The immigrant barracks were adjacent to where the vulture men landed for their payoffs, and there was no way to keep that many people hidden from them, especially considering the children's noise. As far as the vulture men were concerned, that was our problem, not theirs.

Because of this, tribute day had become a little less informal, as Deeplacers and immigrants bumped elbows with each other. Both groups tended to lurk around the windows of the upper levels, watching the arrival and departure of the vulture men. The immigrants in particular were interested, as they had less familiarity with the vulture men.

I was one of the early risers, as I wanted to watch the exchange. Ever since I'd started listening in on the vulture men, matching their voices to faces had become a bit of an obsession. I couldn't get close enough to hear distinct voices or what was being said because the exchange was a good fifty or sixty yards away from the stronghold, but I could observe and match any information gleaned from body language and the interaction with the exchange on the vulture man's end. It was an imperfect system, but it had helped me identify all of the vulture men engaged in the exchange over the past four months.

Despite the labors of preceding days, I greeted this month's tribute day with more relish than normal; Marilyn had gifted me the use of a parabolic microphone with headset. Since learning of my bug and the advantages it had given us, she thought I could use the microphone to get even more information. She figured that since I'd put together a pretty good profile of the vulture men's behavior and opinions with the resources I had, more access would only improve things.

Although she didn't explicitly say it, I suspect Marilyn neglected to tell Abigail about her gift. Abigail preferred that everyone except herself know as little as possible, which was my natural preference as well, but that didn't lessen the irritation of being on the receiving end of my own philosophy. Fortunately, Marilyn was more collaborative; she thought we'd all make better decisions if everyone knew as much as possible. She had the mind of a scientist.

I set up in the smallest room with a window that faced the outer courtyard. It wasn't much larger than a closet and was filled with lumber and odd bits of maintenance supplies. I pulled the curtain tight behind me, blocking out as much backlight as possible, and aimed the microphone receiver toward Abigail and Grendel as they waited for the incoming vulture men. Beside them were five burlap bags filled with various goods—the tribute.

"I hate this," Abigail said.

"I know, but if things go as planned, this is the last time we have to give them real tribute," Grendel soothed. "Stonewall's plan has been executed well, and soon we'll be free of these blood suckers."

"He did do well, didn't he?" I would have liked there to have been less surprise in her voice.

"Yeah, his heart's in the right place. He just doesn't trust anyone, so it seems like he's not thinking things through." The giant continued, "But I doubt if he can even take a piss without thinking about how to 'achieve the objective in the most efficient manner.'"

Abigail laughed. "You should hear what goes on in that rattlebox he calls a brain: plan after plan, contingency within contingency. His thoughts are as convoluted as the gears in the back of a pocket watch. Being around his brain too long puts me on edge, so I have to tune him out or get a headache."

One of the main drawbacks of spying is you hear what other people really think of you. Joke's on them, however. I took her comment as a compliment. I am a thorough guy, and it never hurts to have several back-up plans when things go pear-shaped. The proof's in the pudding—I'm still around to annoy people, aren't I?

Grendel's massive hand lightly patted her shoulder in commiseration. "He's trying even when you can't read his mind, so I can only imagine. But I do know he'd be proud of being considered difficult; he'd wear it like a badge, I suspect."

I swear to God...

She snickered again. "Oh hells yes!" They both chuckled until the vulture men were about to land.

The sound of flapping wings made me dial down the volume, and I missed the first bit of the Linda Jeannette Robickow's introduction, "...come to collect our monthly dividend. Read the list of items so we know we are being paid what is owed."

Both Abigail and Grendel bowed, and Abigail pulled out a list of the tribute items. She had two lists, one which she kept and one which the vulture men took to verify the contents of the bags against once they got home. As Abigail read an item off the list, Grendel would pull it out of a bag and show it to the vulture men, who would then mark it as "received" on their list. I'd never precisely known how much the vulture men wanted in tribute, but as Abigail ran down the list, I realized why she wanted to get out from under them. The vulture men were taking about twenty-five to thirty gold eagles' worth of goods in this exchange, and if that was typical, it was a hefty price indeed. Two gold eagles would get you a musket and enough shot and powder for twenty uses, or an entire box of shotgun shells for a modern shotgun. Well, it used to before the war started up north and drove the prices of weapons and ammunition through the roof.

Abigail finished the list and handed it over to the Linda Jeannette Robickow to double-check against Deeplac's list. The vulture man carefully checked each item on Abigail's list to make sure it matched their list. He signed Abigail's list as the final proof that Deeplac had paid the tribute as indicated on the receipt, and handed it back to her.

"We find this tribute acceptable," the Robickow squawked. "I have been entrusted by the Board of Directors to inform you of a temporary change in our tribute system. The William Howard Spence III has died, and two vie for his position. Because of this, your tribute will be double for the next quarter, as it would be unfair to our two potential great leaders to not treat them with all the respect and dignity of their potential position. We trust you understand and agree to this temporary change, as we have long been business partners and a separation of our interests at this juncture would prove most inadvisable."

The Robickow waited for a response, and he looked confused when none was immediately forthcoming.

Abigail paused, looking at the Robickow and at the other vulture men, and then spoke. "You know what, Grendel?" she said, turning her head to look at the giant behind her and on her left.

"What?" he answered, perplexed by her question.

"I'm really tired of this," she confessed, turning back to the vulture men. "I'm done paying these squawking parasites with the efforts of my people." From the breast pockets of her light jacket flew six razor-sharp disks of metal, silencing the vulture men before they could react to her insult. They flopped on the ground of the outer courtyard, helplessly bleeding out from their lacerated throats, fruitlessly attempting to staunch the red tide with their clawed hands.

Well, I didn't see that one coming, nor did I have a contingency plan for it. As the audible gasps of shock from all the watchers on the lower levels poured through the open windows of the stronghold, I turned up the dial to hear what was said on the ground.

Abigail took a deep and satisfying breath. "I've wanted to do that for soooo long." She turned to Grendel. "If you would grab the tribute and carry it back to the stronghold, I've got to address Deeplac. Things have changed for the better."

Grendel grabbed all the bags of tribute and followed her as she forcefully strode toward the stronghold. I watched Broagh come out of the main doors, undoubtedly speaking to her in his unique way. I wanted to get downstairs for the announcement, so I tucked the parabolic microphone and headset on top of a cabinet where it couldn't be seen and rushed to the ground floor. On my way down, Broagh started the address with a wide broadcast so that all sentients within the stronghold could hear. I stopped on the stairs to listen.

This is Broagh, broadcasting the words of Abigail. Today we have declared our independence from the tyranny of the vulture men. For too long, we have paid them with the hard labor of each one of us, and today we have said, "No More!"

The weapons we have uncovered from the rubble will be our shield against their depredations. If they come to attack us, we will shoot them out of the sky and they will come no more. If they threaten our community, we will make them pay.

But we must exercise caution in our declaration. We do not want them to know what has happened here. If you speak of today to anyone outside these walls, let it be said that we paid as always. Everyone saw the vulture men fly away today, carrying our bags of tribute as they have done every month for years. Everyone needs to keep this secret, for the longer it takes them to realize they are at war, the stronger we will be. The longer it takes them to realize they are no longer our masters, the more time we have to prepare for their attack.

I continued down the stairs as I suspected that Abigail would want to see me, and I didn't have to wait long. As soon as Broagh saw me amidst the crowd leaving the stronghold, he told me to head to the council chamber. I looked out the main doors and saw a crew dragging the vulture men's corpses to the south—probably to bury them in one of the many holes along the southern wall.

Arthur, Morien, and Marilyn were already there by the time I arrived, and Grendel and Broagh entered mere moments after me. Unlike prior visits, I actually had a chair to sit in, so I plopped down and waited with the rest. No one said anything. Morien was talking to herself again, but this time I couldn't be sure if it was to the residents of the otherworld or processing recent events. Abigail arrived in less than a minute. She sat down heavily with a loud exhalation and addressed the room.

"I'm sure you're all stunned, and I know you all wish I would have spoken to you earlier. For that, I have to ask your forgiveness. You, more than any other sentients in the community, know that I would never put my desires over the desires of Deeplac, but that's precisely what I have done today. I have done things this way for decades now and I am fed up with it all. Bluntly, I am never going to pay tribute to any group that does not contribute to the safety of Deeplac. Never again.

"Since Stonewall's discovery of the rifles, the vulture men can't effectively target us. We will proceed with the plan to rebuff Oshkosh's emissaries if they come later today, but I'll honestly be surprised if they even send a tribute request this month. The raiders have cut through the middle of Oshkosh; can they even break through to do so? I don't think they can.

"So this is what's going to happen next: the vulture men will send a follow-up mission to find out what happened to their entire HR Department, and I will show them our receipt signed by the Linda Jeannette Robickow. They will be uncertain how to respond. Given their rigid thinking patterns, they'll feel obligated to honor their word, and we shouldn't have to pay tribute again until the two competing parties show up. We'll then follow through with Stonewall's plan and hand over a token to each faction.

"As discussed earlier, that provides us with enough time to mount more digging missions and hopefully find even more weaponry. We have enough now, but more will always be useful. The month after that, I repeat my little stunt until the vulture men catch on to the idea that we're at war and attack.

"I think it's possible that I may be able to take out three, perhaps four more groups of vulture men in this manner. They're so confident that we're utterly compliant to their wishes; I'm going to take out a sixth of their population before they even figure out what's going on."

A big, evil grin crossed my face as she finished. It was a good plan, a plan that would sow confusion within a colony of vulture men already in disharmony due to the lack of leadership. Everyone else was taken aback by her calm proposal for reasoned bloodthirstiness, even though they'd known her for many years and must have seen this side of her before. I suppose I just accepted this part of her easier than they did. Takes one to know one, I guess. Call me suspicious, but the presence of a chair for me, a chair that hadn't ever been available before, led me to believe that her "impulsive" action was anything but.

"That's a good strategy," I agreed. "I've been working on a way of getting rid of the vulture men for good, if you're interested. Perhaps we could dovetail the two plans together and have a right proper comeuppance for that bunch of gangsters?"

All eyes turned toward me.

"Go on," Abigail requested.

Chapter Seven

Locked In, Locked On, Locked Out

The next night found me sitting on an oak limb some thirty feet above the ground. It was a breezy warm night, a nice summer evening that my counter-shock suit and my adaptive ghillie suit turned into a sweaty, uncomfortable one. The first part of our coordinated plan was my least favorite, as it involved the most personal risk for the least benefit: I was tasked with clearing out the insane robots that patrolled the forests east of Deeplac during the night. I'd argued against it, but the council was adamant, so I ended up here.

The robots were Grynartis 201Fs, manufactured in the Dodoma Robot Works in Tanzania. Used as police robots, the Grynartis African models were free-floating robots designed to engage with electrical force, stunning at the slightest indication of non-compliance, with the ability to apply a lethal charge for more serious infractions. They could detect and identify DNA via a pulsating purple-orange laser system, had excellent night vision, and could see into the infrared for hidden pursuit purposes.

They were only in use for about a decade before recalled

and the program canceled altogether. A hacker compromised the entire Grynartis Automatic Police system, causing dozens of fatalities and costing hundreds of millions in dark-money settlement costs. The hacker was a member of The Company tasked with discrediting the concept of artificial police; you couldn't bribe or blackmail police robots like you could people, and The Company brooked no interference in its long-term African plans. I knew the guy who wrote the hacks; some of the real malfunctions were brutal, and those weren't the ones reported in the media. The news reports were heavily sanitized and any family members or loved ones who refused payment or spoke out disappeared.

Which leads us back to why I'm hanging out on an oak tree; I'm trying to get some people free of the bad guys and this is what being one of the good guys means. I'd spent several decades as a bad guy—admittedly much of that time in cryosleep—and I had a lot to make up for.

I know what you're thinking: why there are African police robots in the Midwest? Your guess is as good as mine.

I'd encountered one of the police robots right after crawling out of my cryopod, and if I didn't have my M1B blaster, I wouldn't have made it past my first day beneath the shattered moon. Thankfully, I knew Swahili—the robots were programmed to use the Tanzanian codes of law enforcement engagement and all vocal commands used the local vernacular—so I was able to comply with its commands, the only reason I wasn't immediately tasered before I could draw my blaster. Otherwise, I would have been captured and dragged off somewhere presumably to die—those who go missing in this area are never seen again.

The only reason I agreed to this part of the plan was the counter-shock suit the tinkers made for me at Abigail's behest. It should ground all non-fatal types of electrical attacks, protecting me from stun guns of all sorts. Fatal levels of electricity would still get through, but I had a chance to survive them, depending on how powerful they were. Marilyn was unhappy with Abigail's request—she's very parsimonious when she makes items that require purple goo to work. She didn't want to "waste" her pupil's rare goos to make a hyper-specific suit that has almost no market value, but acquiesced when Elissa appealed to her sense of duty. "Do you want Stonewall to fry over a few pieces of lavender and lilac tech?" Personally, I think Elissa really wanted to make the suit; her flare for invention when it came to her nanobots bordered on artistic, as opposed to Marilyn's scientific approach.

Additionally, I had free rein of Deeplac's limited collection of high-tech items, which I hoped would be enough to tilt the odds solidly in my favor. I sent out the silvery egg to map the surrounding area for a thorough scan, and I didn't expect it back for an hour. The egg's holographic maps would be invaluable, allowing me to compare the terrain to my maps. In particular, I was looking for the condition of the various police stations in the area, under the assumption that the police robots were based out of one of the stations.

The soft whine of the egg's return drew me out of my reverie. I grabbed the egg and checked its holographic map of the area, focusing on where the old police stations used to be. After a minute of comparing maps, I found Lake Villa Police Station No. 2, with one of the robots moving out of the building and to the east. Well that narrowed things down nicely! I may be ascribing too much logic to this crazy world, but it follows that if police robots were going in and out of a building a mile away from me that happened to be an old police station, there was a good chance the hub was there. The egg had also captured two other robots on its long scan; they were north of Station 2 at the time of the scan, so I had some leeway.

When the council tasked me with destroying the robots, they wanted me to take out the individual robots, but I suggested going after the command and recharge hub. If I destroyed the hub, they would lose contact with command and simply hover in place until they ran out of power or were destroyed.

I carefully climbed down the tree and started toward the station. It was north of me, a little over a mile away, so I quietly hustled in its direction, stopping every five minutes to throw the egg up for nearly real-time reconnaissance. It was hot and tense, but the adaptive ghillie suit should dull my heat signature, blunting me into an indistinct heat source. The tinkers had applied the scent-scrubbing spray Marilyn used to control her night emissions, which should prevent me from leaving a DNA trail. I was guessing on that last bit, but it was an informed one shared by Marilyn and Elissa—the only way the nanobots could remove odors required complete destruction of all particles down to their constituent elements. I should be practically invisible to the robots, or at least invisible enough to shoot them before they knew I was there.

This hypervigilance turned a mile walk into a thirty-minute affair, but it got me where I needed to be without detection. I paused a block south of the station to run a final scan of the nearby exterior with the egg. When it came back clean, I had it scan the interior of the police station—no sense going in blind. I was relieved when it came back after a few minutes; the interior couldn't have been that big.

I turned on the map and searched for the hub. The upper level was relatively intact and looked much like any police station from the late twenty-first century. I hurriedly glanced over the upper level offices and storage rooms before finding the hub nestled in the EMP-hardened center of the station. Bingo!

I shut down the map, returned the egg to my side pocket, and headed into the station as quickly as I could. I wanted to get this done before any of the robots came back. It shouldn't take me more than five minutes to get in, destroy the control center with my plasma cutter, and then get out. Once I was out, I'd run the egg again, and relocate the three robots to see if they were neutralized. They should be floating in place, bereft of will and direction once the hub was down.

I knew I'd messed up the moment I passed through the open double doors of the station. The egg was a great source of information, but it didn't prevent user error. I had failed to check the lower level maps before barging in like a drunk rhino, and the wretched smell within the station alerted me that this was a place of death.

I quickly retreated to my prior hiding place to review the lower level maps. The area was a lock-up where prisoners served time for minor sentences or waited before being transferred to more long-term facilities. I stared at the hologram for several seconds before I could grasp what the egg had recorded. There were twenty to thirty different holding cells for the station, each of them filled with corpses in various states of decay.

There were hundreds, perhaps thousands of corpses. Some of the cells were so packed it was impossible to fit any more within them. The robots were just throwing the sentients they captured into the cells, but they weren't programmed to take care of the detained. Apparently, there was nothing in their programming that prohibited throwing living beings into piles of putridity in which no normal creature would be able to survive for very long.

I started searching the cells for danger or scavengers, and in the process caught a blurred image amidst the corpses in the farthest cell. There was someone alive down there! Only moving things left blurred images in the egg's hologram.

I shoved the egg back in my pocket and raced into the station, putting on one of the gas masks I'd pilfered during Marilyn's rescue from the rat men. I didn't know how bad the air was going to get, and the gas mask gave me a modicum of protection.

Flashlight in hand, I sped down the stairs, taking them three at a time. I rounded the first landing but lost my footing on an unexpectedly slick step. I landed hard in something wet, and my flashlight skittered down the remainder of the flight. I recovered quickly, retrieving my light.

I illuminated my ghillie suit pants—I'd slipped in fresh blood. The robot leaving the station on the first scan must have just dropped a prisoner off. I wiped the blood off my hands as best I could and continued to the first lock point. I pulled out my plasma cutter and sliced through it, working my way to the second lock point where I did the same.

I entered the main holding area and the immensity of the horror hit me. How many years had this been going on? How many hundreds or thousands of sentients spent their last days in the dark surrounded by rotting corpses, their living bodies covered in slime and maggots? I tried not to think about it as I trod to the far cell, stepping over the arm bones that littered the hallway, the extended limbs of those who'd died trying to get out. As I went, I used my plasma cutter to cut the locks of every chamber ensuring that regardless of the outcome of my mission, this atrocity ended here.

I reached the final cell, and my flashlight revealed the terrified brown face of a human-looking kid staring back at me; she couldn't have been more than six. I tried to talk as I slid the plasma cutter through the lock, but realized I probably looked like a monster in my ghillie suit and gas mask. I put my cutter away, pulled off the mask and the ghillie hood, and immediately lost my lunch after my first inhale.

Some rescuer I am.

I regained control of myself as fast as I could. "I'm here to get you out of here, kid," I said with as much confidence as I could muster while I reached for her. The kid didn't move as I grabbed her arm. Instead, she pointed at a nearby fresh corpse of a woman.

I shook my head. "Sorry kiddo, she didn't make it."

The kid nodded. "She wants me to tell you something."

I stopped cold.

"She wants me to tell you that if you hurt me, she'll eat you while you sleep."

The hair on my arms and neck stood up. "I'm not going to hurt you. I'm going to take you home where there are hundreds of sentients to take care of you," I said.

"Okay, you'd better hurry; the angry things want you"—she waved her arms back and forth at the body-filled cells—"and they won't wait much longer." She raised her arms for me to pick her up.

I grabbed her, carrying her with my left arm while holding the gas mask and ghillie hood in the same hand. I didn't run, given the obstacles littering the floor, but I moved as fast as I could go without falling. I felt like I was being watched as I went, like I was stealing a precious bit of treasure from right under the nose of a sleeping dragon. I had the persistent sense that something was going to reach out and grab me from behind.

The pressure alleviated when we made it to the stairwell, but I'm certain I heard something moving in the cellblock as we reached the landing where I'd previously slipped. That was the last straw for me, and I let my monkey mind free, fleeing the place where the monsters lurked as fast as I could. I was just outside the double doors of the station when I remembered the robots.

"I'm sorry, kid. I gotta go back. I have to destroy the machines that killed your mom," I said, looking down at her bloody face, trying to hide the fear in my voice. I did not want to go back in there.

She nodded and I turned back in, moving as quickly as I could to the EMP-sheltered center of the ground level. Even before I entered the room, I saw the glow of flashing green, yellow, and red lights emanating from the machinery within. Turning and entering, I was greeted by four working charge stations surrounding a large bank of still-operative computers.

"Stand right here for a second, okay?" I told the kid as I set her down. I quickly stuffed my gas mask and ghillie suit hood into my pack. I pulled my plasma cutter out, picked up the flashlight, and started cutting through every cable in the room. Once that was done and all the flashing lights were no longer flashing, I cut through the metal sections of the recharging station, ensuring that they couldn't be rebuilt without extreme effort.

This took less than a minute. The kid kept inching deeper into the room, away from the entrance as I went about my business, a sure sign that we really needed to leave. I stashed the cutter, grabbed the kid with my left arm—hand holding the flashlight—and pulled out my M1B in case I was too late for a clean escape.

I paused, standing completely still, before leaving the room to listen. The sound of slow plodding footsteps broke the silence, its echo revealing its location at the stairwell. At least it was on my right side; I'd be between it and the kiddo, whatever it was.

I broke my stance with haste, holding the girl as tightly as I felt was safe. I dashed south toward the stairwell and the double doors that were our way out. There was a shadowy figure on the stairwell. I immediately shot at it, a red blast of plasma spurting from the end of the M1B. The destructive crimson bolt illuminated its path and I caught my first glimpse of our pursuer: a mass of severed heads held together in a roughly humanoid shape.

The plasma holed the center of its "chest," tunneling through to impact the wall behind. The spirit-made-flesh stumbled from the blast, and I bolted past it, flying through the double doors in a heartbeat. I now had sixty-four shots left. I didn't know if it had any lasting effect upon the creature—I kept running for several blocks before slowing down to a walk.

The kid pulled on my arm and calmly said, "You shouldn't stop."

I turned to look—a swarm of flying eyeballs made chase, glowing green and red in the darkness.

I sprinted and the little one reflexively tightened her hold on me. I ran faster than I should, trusting the strength of my ankles and boots to keep me on my feet, hoping for a streak of blind luck. Fear propelled me to the forest line without injury.

I gazed back and didn't see anything. Breathing heavily, I put the girl down. "What's your name?"

"Efte."

"Hello Efte, I'm William." I reached down for a handshake, which she tentatively reciprocated. "I live in a place called Deeplac—"

"That's where we were heading when the metal monster got us," she interrupted.

"You and your mother were heading to Deeplac?"

"And Dad, but they killed him 'cause he didn't like what they did to Mom. The twitching thing that made her go to sleep."

I nodded. "I'm sorry about your parents. I'll get you there, and there are a lot of good sentients there who will take care of you."

"Promise?"

"I promise," I affirmed, crossing my heart with my right hand.

Chapter Eight

A New Home

I hoisted Efte up into my arms once the egg verified that no, the ghastly severed-head monster wasn't coming after us and that yes, the Grynartis 201Fs were frozen in place, bereft of direction. A scavenging crew would come to collect them tomorrow during the day; Marilyn made it quite clear that she wanted to get her furry paws on them before approving my mission.

Efte was silent for the trip, clinging onto my ghillie suit like a baby capuchin as we made our way through the forest; the fabric designed for concealment and camouflage turned me into an incidental giant teddy bear. I had the feeling she was a quiet kid by nature, not that there was much to say after what we had seen. The periodic squirm and lack of slow rhythmic breathing let me know she was still awake as we made our way into the clearing surrounding Deeplac.

We were about halfway across the field when the gate guards challenged us, "Halt! Who goes there?"

Yes, that's really what they said.

"It is I, William Stonewall of Deeplac, returning from a

night mission!" Might was well ham it up if they're going to be so ridiculous. They didn't seem to notice.

"Stonewall! Come on in!"

I approached the gates and the keeper looked down at me. "Who's the kid?"

"Her name's Efte. I rescued her. She's living with us now."

The gates creaked open and I walked through. The keeper met us at the entrance.

"Seems like you're always carrying something when you arrive late at night"—he referenced the liobear carcass I had on my back the last time—"but I like this one better." He bent down and gave Efte a pat on her head. "Welcome to Deeplac."

We passed through and he closed and barred the gate behind us. I went to the stronghold and knocked on the doors for entrance. The sliding peephole opened; I identified myself and was let in.

"Any of the elders up?" I asked the door guard.

"Arthur may be in the kitchen. At least he was the last time I made rounds," the guard responded, eying Efte.

"I'll check there first, then. Thanks," I said to the guard on my way to the kitchen. The kid probably wanted some food anyway…who knows how long it's been since she ate. She was on the skinny side; not malnourished, but I could tell she'd skipped a meal or two in her recent past.

"Are you hungry?" I asked her.

I could feel her nod against my shoulder.

"Let's get you some hot soup."

I walked into the kitchen, but there was no sign of Arthur. A few other sentients were talking quietly and eating by lamp light. One of them was a group of younger Deeplacers that included Reginald. I interrupted their conversation, face brooking no discussion.

"Reginald, this is Efte. I rescued her from a bad situation tonight and I need to wake one of the elders to talk about it. You all need to watch her for a few minutes. Get her as much soup as she wants and tell the cook to break out one of the small pots of honey," I ordered. "You can share in the honey as well," I said to the group, "just take care of her."

Reginald nodded while one of the others got up to notify the cook. I looked at Efte. "You gotta let go of me. I want you meet my friend Reginald—he will make sure you get as much food as you can eat." She reluctantly released her hold; the lure of food was strong enough, and the pleasing aroma from the kitchen helped. I set her on one of the benches. "I'll be right back with someone very special. I think you'll like her."

I went to rouse Morien. As a member of the elder council, she had a private bedroom, but hers had one of the few actual doors in the stronghold besides the one to Abigail's chambers. I had always assumed it was to block out the noise of her constant chatter with the otherworld but I could also understand the importance of separating the physical remnants of spirits from the other residents of Deeplac.

I knocked on her door. "Morien, I need to see you. I found a kid on my mission. I think she's a sorcerer."

I heard a bang and a curse from the other side. The door cracked open, and Morien stuck her head out. "You better be serious."

"I'm serious," I assured her.

"Give me a second." The door closed and reopened. She exited wearing a thin nightdress, a big change from her typical thick, tough clothing. "Where's the child?"

I led her down to the kitchen and found the group of youths huddled around Efte. Her hands and face had been wiped down, and she was happily chowing down on bread and honey. I was impressed to find the youths had restrained themselves from the honey until the new arrival had her fill—good kids.

They made space opposite Efte as soon as we entered the kitchen. Morien took a seat after gliding across the room in her white gown. I sat next to her.

"Hello child, I am Morien. I'm going to ask Stonewall to tell us what happened tonight, and then I'm going to ask you some questions about his story."

Efte didn't say anything, but her eyes softened, indicating she understood. She was focused on the honey. I quickly ran through the story up to where we escaped the severed-head spirit. My direct and flat descriptions only heightened the horror for the others, but Efte didn't flinch or show any emotion when I mentioned her dead parents or the chase through the woods.

Trauma can be tricky, especially with young children that you don't know very well beforehand. But she seemed content at the moment, licking the honey off her sticky fingers.

"Efte," Morien addressed her once I'd finished, "can you see the shadow people?"

The small head bobbed up and down.

"Can you tell me how many shadows are following Reginald here?" She indicated the large youth.

Efte held up one hand, three fingers displayed proudly. Reginald's peers shied away from him ever so slowly.

"And him?" Morien nodded in my direction. "How many shadows linger on him?"

"I'm sorry, ma'am," she said quietly, with worry in her voice. "I can't count that high." Shivers ran down my spine as I looked around; everyone except Morien and Efte gave me a wide berth to accommodate my cadre of invisible spirit people.

Morien slipped out a small snort. "That's okay, child. There's a lot of them and you don't have to count that high yet." Efte let out a soft sigh of relief as she finished the piece of bread in her hand.

Morien stood up and addressed the older kids, "I need to talk to Stonewall for a bit." She indicated with her head that I should follow her, and we stepped away from the group.

"So was I right?" I asked.

"Yes, she's a sorcerer. I'm going to have to take her on as an apprentice. You don't want her running around without any guidance—messes will happen."

"Sounds prudent," I agreed. "You want me to grab some bedding for her while you take her to your chamber?"

"That would be nice," she agreed before changing the subject. "It's a good thing you ran away, Stonewall. I have no idea what was following you, what resides in that police station—I've never heard of anything like it. We'll have to put that location off limits for scavenging."

"Running away seemed the smart move at the time. But honestly, I'm not sure I really had much of a choice; the thing filled me terror. Not even the hollow mummy felt like that," I confided, "and that heap of empty undead linen nearly killed us."

She shrugged noncommittally. "If you'd go find the bedding, we'll be in my room."

"Sure. Let me say goodnight and I'll get the stuff."

We returned to the table; the other kids divvying up the remaining honey, slathering it over the remaining bread while Efte stretched and yawned, her small belly pouched.

"Morien's going to take you on as an apprentice. You'll be sleeping in her room tonight."

Her serious brown eyes gazed at the plump black woman in the white dressing gown with braids falling down her back. "Momma wants me to tell you that if you hurt me, she'll eat you while you sleep."

The youths froze, mouths full of honey and bread, eyes

boring into Efte. The room felt heavy, the lights dimmer.

"I know, dear," Morien responded. "I heard her. I'm not going to hurt you. I'm going to teach you how to help people."

Efte made a serious face. "I guess that's what I should do."

Morien held out her hand. "Let's go to bed then. It's very late, and I'm sleepy."

She stood and took her hand. Walking away, I heard Efte say, "It's called a blutgeist. That's what was after us."

Morien stopped and knelt down, bringing her face to the child's. "How do you know this?"

"I…I don't know," Efte tremulously responded.

Morien stared into her eyes, searching for something. I don't know if she found it, but after an uncomfortable moment, she rose and guided the girl to her room.

"Don't forget to bring the bedding, Stonewall."

Chapter Nine

Training Day

It took the vulture men on the Board of Directors three days before they reached an agreement to send an investigatory mission to Deeplac. Because the Board held their meetings in the main meeting area where my bug clung to the ceiling, I was privy to their internal debate. One group believed Deeplac and the other communities had engaged in some sort of—and I quote—"tomfoolery," another believed that the Linda Jeannette Robickow had been waylaid by an external force sometime during his tribute gathering, and a third believed the Robickow had staged some sort of minor coup, flying off to who knows where with the loot.

I kept Abigail informed of the discussions, so when the day came, she and Broagh were prepared. They spent their time close to Deeplac's gates, which remained unusually closed during the daylight hours. She also put up a triple guard, but she kept the newly recovered rifles out of sight under tarps along the gate walk.

When the cry of "Horcs!" went up from the gate, Broagh told all the sentients of Deeplac to seek shelter via a wide broadcast. They had to scurry to make it, but everyone took refuge from any potential dropped rocks by the time the vulture men appeared in the sky. According to the vulture men's plan, the horcs were to remain far enough within the forest to remain unseen. However, horcs and subtly do not mix, and they were easily detected, as anticipated.

I dashed back to the closet I used previously to eavesdrop on tribute day. Despite her better judgment, Marilyn let me keep the parabolic microphone stashed in the closet, knowing that I couldn't carry it around with me nor could I rely on her or Elissa being available when I needed it. It took some sweet-talking, but she came around, at least until the issue with the vulture men was decided. I managed to get the headphones on and mic turned in the right direction by the time the vulture men landed.

"Greetings Abigail, ruler of Deeplac!" one of the vulture men announced once they had settled. "I am the Conner Twinefil Cabot, Board Member, and I come regarding your late payment of tribute." His beak was bent at the culmen, resulting in a gap between the upper and lower mandibles; he tended to spray spittle as he talked.

"Greetings, the Conner Twinefil Cabot! I welcome you to Deeplac, but I am confused by what you mean regarding a late payment. We paid the Linda Jeannette Robickow three days ago in the same manner as we always have," Abigail responded.

"We have not seen the tribute, Abigail!" the bent-beaked

birdman hissed. Again, part of their plan—an attempt to intimidate. Negotiations were easier when you knew what the other side was planning to do; good intel made life predictable.

"We have this receipt, the Conner Twinefil Cabot," Abigail said as she withdrew the receipt from one of her pockets. "The Linda Jeannette Robickow also informed us of the double tribute for the next quarter after she found our tribute acceptable." She handed the receipt to the vulture man. "I'd assumed that the first double tribute would occur at the typical appointed time and location?"

The vulture man nodded yes to her question and studied the receipt. "This looks in order," he conceded once he finished reading it. After waiting a painful second, he acquiesced, "We will accept this as proof of payment. Deeplac has a long record of timeliness. Surely this is just some clerical error we will correct shortly."

He hissed at the other vulture men, and they took to their wings without saying goodbye. They flew to the south instead of the east; probably going to other communities to see if they'd paid tribute as well. The conflicting accounts would puzzle them and make them suspicious, but what solid conclusion could they reach? They didn't have enough actionable information yet.

Once the vulture men were out of sight, Broagh broadcast to Deeplac to return to normal. He must have said something privately to Abigail right afterward, because she started laughing and almost clapped him on the back before stopping herself short of his spines.

I left the closet and returned the parabolic microphone and headset to Marilyn. I wasn't going to need it for another month and she would rest easier knowing it was back in her care. She and Elissa were my link to what passes for science and technology here, so I always went out of my way to keep them happy. Plus, the good-faith return increased my chances of borrowing other equipment from her in the future, like a library for gearheads that runs on goodwill.

I grabbed some lunch, sitting silently next to Morien and Efte. They had been inseparable since the young girl's arrival. I didn't know if that was a typical master-apprentice relationship for sorcerers, but it was working well for Efte. She was comfortable around her newly adopted family. Morien appeared a bit more harried than before, but that was to be expected. Kids wore you down, even the quiet, introverted ones like Efte. It was nice to see Morien talking to someone physically there for a change.

"I've been meaning to ask what you meant by shadows following me?"

It took a second for Morien to realize I was talking to her. "Huh?"

"When you first spoke with Efte, you mentioned shadows following Reginald and me," I reminded her.

"Oh, yeah. Those are all the sentients you've killed. They

follow you around," she said disinterestedly, as if responding to a question about the weather.

"Do they...um...do anything?"

"Not normally. Every now and then, they can get rambunctious."

"Rambunctious?"

"Move stuff around. Make you lose something," she answered. "Most of the time it's petty and inconvenient, but sometimes it can be fatal. Spoke with a spirit once whose shadows pushed the key of a strong room under the door, trapping him within. He died, in time."

"So you're saying that everyone I've ever killed is following me around, and they're pissed at me?"

She turned, looking me square on. "Well, what the hell do you expect if you go around killing people? They just disappear and you're free?" She started snicker. Even Efte giggled a little.

"It's doesn't work that way, Stonewall. They're yours now. You claimed them. They're with you until you're put down or until you make peace with them. And frankly, you're not the peacemaking type. They will know if you really mean it. You wouldn't." The hint of judgment mixed with satisfaction in her voice was a rare thing for one normally so indifferent.

Well, that's just great.

"What about the blutgeist?" I asked.

Morien shot me a stare. "I won't speak of that. Good day, Stonewall." She abruptly ended our conversation and hurriedly grabbed her and Efte's dishes before retreating into the depths of the stronghold. They were gone before I could eke out a protest. "Was it something I said?"

It wasn't the first time I had finished lunch alone and probably wouldn't be the last. I was out of my depth with otherworld stuff and clearly the sorcerers were not open to a discussion about this particular spirit. There was something going on there, but I didn't have time to dwell on it. Now that Abigail had successfully convinced the vulture men that tribute was paid, it was time to move on to the next step—training, both as a student and an instructor.

I glommed onto the spear quickly upon my arrival, but I needed more training and looked forward to Zew's class after lunch. He only took the best as students, and when I didn't quite make the cut, I built him a training field and the free labor tipped him to my favor. I had cleared out a circle, roughly forty feet in diameter, leveled it off with dirt, and placed large stones around its circumference where observers could sit and learn from those engaged in combat within. Next to the circle was a barrel containing a score of practice spears that I had blunted and dulled.

Zew and Diana stood outside the ring while the students picked their practice spears from the barrel. Diana didn't need lessons, but she was always there and they trained against each other, as they were the only two in the community that provided "good sport" to each other, as she liked to say. I arrived just before spear class started, grabbing a weapon. As I sat down, Zew spoke.

"You're all here because you're the best in Deeplac," he said, looking over the eight sentients before him. "But that's not saying much for some of you." He looked at me, which elicited some chuckles. "My goal is to get you to the point where you can competently train others. We have four weeks to get there."

"My teaching method is simple and direct," he continued as he walked to the barrel, grabbed a spear for himself and a second that he tossed to Diana. "You fight against me until you get better. You will watch me fight others until you get better. Each of you will have different strengths and weaknesses, and I expect you to learn from your mistakes as well as the mistakes of others. Stonewall, let's start with you since you need the most work."

The rest of the two-hour session was a blur of rapid thwacks, barked critiques, and a mass of bruises upon all of us. Even Diana got her ass handed to her, but she grinned the whole time, like it was friendly game of badminton. Zew would have corrected that behavior in any of us, but there was little point in correcting Diana. She was a breed of her own, and you didn't mess with her style.

One thing I learned was that Zew doesn't tire like normal sentients. He fought all of us in a series over a two-hour period, and at the end, he seemed to be in roughly the same condition as when he began. He didn't show any of the bent-back weariness that should come after such a strenuous effort. His breathing was a little more rapid and heavy, but like a boxer in round three, not in round twelve. His multi-colored mohawk didn't even deflate. The more I learned about him, the more I understood why he'd survived the wastelands.

The next two hours were nearly the reverse of the prior. I was the instructor, the subject was riflery, and no one would be nursing bruises tomorrow morning. Now that we had a slew of rifles available for our defense, I needed to train all those unfamiliar with the weapon. Several of Deeplac's former musketeers needed instruction on the weapon upgrade, as did many of the diggers who found themselves unexpected rifle owners; even those familiar with the weapon needed instructions on using them with scopes, something which Deeplac had previously lacked.

Along with creating the spear-training circle, I'd spent the past few days setting up two shooting ranges about a quarter mile north of the northern wall: one for the rifles and one for the muskets. It had taken quite a bit of effort, but Deeplac now had a 50-, 100-, 200-, 300-, and 400-yard firing range. Each range had three firing lines, the fifty-yard firing line only for musketeers or complete novices with a rifle.

I had twelve students new to the modern rifle but familiar with the musket, so all they really needed was a solid grounding in the differences in use and some quality time at the range. Ammunition was the limiting factor in the post-apocalypse;

every round of ammunition used in practice was a round not available when needed during an attack. I allotted each gunner ten shots after I zeroed in their sights, and we did each shot serially, trying to maximize the teaching opportunity from each emptied cartridge. All in all, the group did passably well and everyone felt comfortable with their new weapons by the end of the session. They would have to learn by doing from this point forward.

The last hour of my training day went quickly. I was familiar with the use of muskets, and I could, given enough time, load and fire them, but I was far from proficient. I should have started training with them earlier, but I held out hope that I would never be in a situation requiring knowledge of them. That hope seemed more in vain the longer I stayed beneath the shattered moon. It would be better to know and never need, than need and not know. Admittedly, there was a bit of pride in my reluctance—I didn't want to go to a "lesser" firearm than the ones I was familiar with.

I got over it.

Unlike the rifles we'd dug up, we had enough supplies of musket powder and shot to allow us a full hour's practice, firing in quick succession. By the end of the hour, I could reliably fire two rounds per minute. However, I had plenty of room to improve—Drat, the instructor, could fire five per minute.

After the musket training, I carried the barrel full of blunt spears back inside Deeplac's gates and deposited it along the interior wall. I grabbed some dinner and headed to my room; there were still a few hours of light left, but it'd been a tough day and I needed to go through my daily recordings of the vulture men.

Most of the recording was tripe, but I caught a nugget of information at the very end that set my brain reeling. I needed to speak to the council again. Assembling them took a bit of time as Deeplac was abuzz with activity on all fronts. It wasn't until after lunch the following day that we gathered in the council chamber. Notably absent was the chair I sat in last time.

"Can't you go a week without causing a fuss?" Arthur asked when he finally arrived. With the southern wall finished in haste to hide the dead vulture men, he'd moved on trenching out star-like expansions on the western and northern walls; Abigail had decided to expand the territory within the palisade and there wasn't any digging in Deeplac that didn't include Arthur. He always grumbled, but he was there when it needed doing.

"Sorry Arthur, but this is really something you should hear," I said to the dusty bipedal armadillo as he took his specially crafted seat; it wasn't comfortable sitting in a normal seat when you're covered in a thick shell, although he could manage for short stints.

"All right, what's this about?" Abigail probed as Arthur settled in.

"Yesterday while reviewing the vulture-men recordings, I overheard the Hayden Miles Dannavant, one of the vulture men competing for CEO, plot to take the horcs on a raid against the rat men. Apparently, they didn't kill and eat the rat man that I handed over several months ago like they threatened to do; they got maps of Gurn Ills Mall out of him and he has agreed to stage a surprise attack for the horcs in exchange for his life and freedom. Not a bad deal for him, considering I thought he would have been dead within the week."

"Was there information on a timeline?" Grendel inquired.

"I didn't hear anything specific, but I'd think it would be something he'd choose to do earlier rather than later, in light of the competition. If it ends up failing, he will have time to recover from it before the quarter is over."

"If they stage a surprise attack…how many horcs are there?" Marilyn asked of me.

"I saw more than twenty when I took the rat man in. I'd assume at least an equal number were elsewhere when I arrived, so at least forty, but perhaps up to sixty or so. I don't think there's more than that.

"If they go in with forty horcs and surprise, I think they just might be able to dig the rat men out," she said. "I only saw two or three dozen rat-men warriors when they dragged me from my cell to inspect their stockpile of technological items." Although some of us had been inside the rat men's mall, none of us had gone further north than Marilyn's cell, and we'd only seen a handful of rat men.

"There were about three dozen warriors in the nest, after the losses they took on their botched raid and after the losses we directly inflicted," Abigail chimed in. Her abilities gave her uncanny insider knowledge from when we used to trade with them before they'd kidnapped Marilyn. "They could have added more since. There are a few smaller communities, spin-offs from the larger band over the years based southeast of the vulture men's territory, from which they could possibly pick up new residents. Unlikely, in my opinion, but possible."

"What would the horcs gain in a successful raid?" Arthur asked Marilyn. "Could they pull out the food machine they had you fix?"

"I don't think so. Unless they've got a tinker, it's not going anywhere," she responded.

"So you could move it?" I asked.

"It would be difficult, and I'd need a lot of physical help, but I could break it up into several parts for transportation. I should be able to put it back together. But that doesn't matter, because we don't have the power to run it."

Power? Broagh broadcast.

"Yeah, I could jury-rig a power source from what we've got, but I'd end up draining all our power cells within a week. It uses a lot of power and it doesn't have its own power supply."

I remembered the dim red lights in the mall. "So there's a generator of some sort down there?"

She nodded. "I don't know what type, but the rat men had a few functioning lights as well as the food machine. When I asked about it, they told me to shut up, so I didn't get anything from them." She paused, thinking. "They seemed more embarrassed than suspicious when I asked. Perhaps they don't really know where the power is coming from?"

"So you're saying that there could be a power source waiting to be found?"

"Well, there is something in there powering the area, so yeah, I guess I am. It would have to be someplace the rats never went. And if they don't know why or how they have power, it would have to be something that doesn't need refueling or something drawing power from a permanent source, like the sun or the earth itself."

"Earth itself?" Arthur's bushy eyebrows rose.

"Geothermal. If you do it right, you can generate electricity using the heat of the earth. It's hard to do and it requires a lot of equipment, but it doesn't require a lot of maintenance."

"It could be a fusion reactor," I said. Marilyn's head went back at my suggestion. "We had some in my time. They were very big, but if it came from some time after my time, it's possible."

"It's always possible. I've only briefly worked with nuclear materials."

The word "nuclear" set off a rustle among the council members. Beneath the shattered moon, "nuclear" was almost always followed by the words "poison," "death," "sickness," or some other variation of general unpleasantness.

"I'm certain we wouldn't want to mess with that," Abigail reassured the room.

"If it is fusion, it's not like what you think nuclear means," Marilyn argued. "It's relatively harmless compared with the benefits it produces."

I could tell Abigail didn't want to argue theoreticals, so she returned to the main subject at hand and reiterated, "So we don't have a timeline for the horc's attack?"

"No," I responded. "But I think this is an opportunity. Regardless who wins, there will be fewer horcs and rat men once the battle is over. I think we should plan an attack of our own, either on the rat men after the horcs fail or against the horcs after they succeed. We have a chance to claim all the materials in the nest for Deeplac, and although I wouldn't recommend it, we'd also have a fallback position if the northern barbarians return powerful enough to really threaten us. Living underground isn't ideal, but it's living, and we'd figure out something to do if we had the time."

"If we do this, we're jumping the timeline—we're letting the vulture men know we're at war with them earlier than we'd previously discussed," Arthur cautioned.

"Definitely," I acknowledged. "We can't be sure how the Hayden Miles Dannavant's raid will pan out. However, if we execute our part of the raid with precision, there may be no survivors to report such a declaration back to the vulture men. I'm not sure how likely that is, but it is a possibility." I looked around the table; all the faces were deep in thought.

"And frankly, I'd be a lot happier with the rest of our plan against the vulture men if I didn't have to sneak through a horde of horcs to pull it off," I added.

"All right," Abigail said, "you've got the job, but I want you to take someone else with you this time. Last time you went alone and got lucky; this time, I'd like you go with some support and less reliance on chance."

"Who do you want to go?"

"That's up to you, but you've got to convince them to go with you in less than an hour. I want you out there with eyes on the Lancaster Building and the rats' nest by tonight. Hope you weren't planning on getting much sleep for the next few days."

Chapter Ten

A Little Birdie Told Me

It took two more hours to nail down the details of the operation, during which time I considered who I wanted to accompany me. Ideally, it would be someone who was a good shot with a fair amount of stamina, and someone I could get along with for a couple of days. Being good with a rifle limited my choices significantly. Drat was good with firearms and his natural camouflage ability would be very useful, but he was not very physical. We might end up having to cover a large distance in a short time, and I doubted he had that kind of endurance. I had to cover almost sixty miles in a single day during my last stint; while the council's plan didn't rely on such mobility, you never knew when things would go pear-shaped and you just needed to run.

That left me with Zew or Diana. Both had the stamina to keep up a moderate pace, were great in melee combat, and tolerated me well enough, but both were only passable shots. By the numbers, Zew was slightly better for the mission, but Diana had saved my skin before and we had a good in-field rapport. I knew Diana better and trusted her more, which pushed her to the top of the list. Trust is important; trust saves your life.

After we had ironed everything out and ended the meeting, I went to the kitchen looking for food and found Diana sitting with Morien and Efte. Grabbing a bowl of soup, I joined their table.

"So Diana," I opened, "I've a mission that I'm supposed to run and wondered if you'd be interested in going with me?"

"When?" she asked bluntly.

"We need to leave in a few hours; sooner, if possible."

"I'm in. Let me get my gear and I'll meet you down here in fifteen minutes."

"Don't you want to know what it is?"

"Nope. You can tell me on the way." She got up, then paused for a second, "Overnight, I take it—need food?"

"I'm packing for four days. May be longer."

"Got it. Make it twenty minutes," she said and left the kitchen.

I looked at Morien and Efte. "She doesn't need much time to make up her mind, does she?"

Efte laughed like I made a great joke, but her face quickly turned serious. "Stop it!" she commanded to the empty space over my left shoulder.

"Be nice," Morien said, touching her apprentice's shoulder.

"Sorry," she apologized to the spot.

"I've told you—the more you talk to them, the more they

talk back. Don't do that to Stonewall; he's in enough trouble on his own."

"Sorry," she repeated, this time directed at me.

"Quite all right, Efte," I said, following about half the conversation.

"How's she doing?" I asked Morien.

"She seems to be adjusting. She wakes up in the night crying, but for her age—for being one of us—that's normal and should pass."

I nodded knowingly, even though I didn't have a clue what it was like being a child that could interact with the otherworld. I knew I wasn't fit to raise children, and I wouldn't have pegged Morien for the maternal type either, but she was taking it in stride and the child seemed happy here with her new guardian. Morien had always been a very private person, so I knew it couldn't be easy on her to have that responsibility thrust upon her so suddenly, but she was the only one capable of addressing Efte's unique situation.

I wolfed down my soup—when Diana said twenty minutes, she meant it. I said my goodbyes and went to gather my stuff. I met up with Diana and we did a gear check, inspecting each other's equipment to make sure both of us thought everything was solid. That was one of the things I liked about her; even though she wasn't a former operative, those sort of things came naturally to her. After mutual agreement that our gear was sound, we picked up travel rations—a post-apocalyptic version of pemmican—from Gormond's pantry, and informed Abigail that we were leaving.

Since it wasn't a scouting mission, Abigail wouldn't let me take the silver egg, but she gave us the communicator. We were supposed to inform her of any changes gathered visually or from my vulture-men bug. I expected to hear about the march before we saw signs of movement, which would give Deeplac plenty of time to maneuver, but worst case, our forces could be at the rats' nest in two hours. It would be a hard march, but they could make a beeline, reducing my normal fifteen-mile trip down to only eleven miles.

We traveled along a familiar path I used every time I moved between Deeplac and the rats' nest: about half the distance in the forest and the other half on what's left of I-94. I-94 was a double-decker, twelve-lane, elevated monstrosity built with plascrete. If you could climb up to the lower deck, you had a nice safe road to travel upon. The upper deck protected you from air-born threats like vulture men or cloudhorses while the elevation protected you from the many ground-based threats, like the ever-present bunnysharks.

As we trekked, I explained the mission to Diana.

"So you can hear them in your head?" she asked after I explained bugging the vulture men's lair.

"Sort of. The computer in my head receives the bug's transmissions. When I listen to them, the signal bypasses my ears and goes straight to the auditory part of my brain. So I'm not actually hearing them but it sounds like I'm hearing them, if you get what I mean."

She shrugged. "Morien hears things none of us can hear all the time, and Broagh talks directly into my head. So it's like that."

"Similar, yes," I responded.

I finished the rest of the mission brief, and she was fully behind any opportunity to take out the rats and grab their loot. She led the team for Marilyn's safe return in exchange for fixing their food machine and she never forgave them for reneging. We walked for another hour in silence before reaching I-94. After climbing up, we headed south and kept to the center of the highway, ensuring that nothing on the ground could see us and minimizing our chances of being seen from the air.

We arrived at our observation point an hour later. It was the same spot I used when surveilling the rat men after Marilyn's kidnapping, but this time we were on the opposite side of I-94 looking east toward the Lancaster Building. Our location was a good choice for most of the day except during part of the morning, when the rising sun would shine directly into our eyes. During that hour, we would have to hide behind one of the barricade pillars, peeking out every few minutes to check for moving horcs.

Using our knives, we cut swaths of the moss growing along the exterior barriers and breaks in the old drainage system where water fed the plants. After an hour of labor, we were rewarded with comfortable mossy seats from which we could see all the lands east of I-94. Then we camouflaged our position, piling the moss into mounds. Only our heads would protrude over the moss, reducing the chance that the sharp-eyed vulture men could see us. With the last of the light, we finished setting up camp. Along with the two mossy sitting areas, we also created two sleeping platforms a few inches off the ground, just high enough to clear the cold damp gray plascrete.

"I'm going to zone out for a bit," I announced. "I need to review the recordings and see if anything's happened. You want to contact Abigail and let her know we're here and set up?"

Diana retrieved the communicator from my pack and had a short communique with Abigail while I checked the recordings, which showed a significant uptick in activity over the past few hours. Had they left already? I wondered.

When Diana hung up, I clued her in on the avian chatter and advised a close watch on the roads leading here while I took the time to listen to every last squawk. She picked up my binoculars and turned toward the road. I'd taught her how to switch between low light and infrared, and I could hear her switch back and forth every few minutes.

It took nearly an hour to plow through all the discussions recorded that day. The only thing of note was that one of the vulture men in contention for the position of CEO, the Preston Hammond Wolcott, Esq., had just returned from leading the horcs on a successful extortion mission against "the underground mushroom people." I didn't get any more information, except that they were to the southeast of the Lancaster Building living in an underground bunker which they'd converted into a giant mushroom cavern.

"Diana, you ever heard about mushroom people living in an underground bunker southeast of here?" I queried.

"No. Why?"

"I just heard one of the vulture men bragging about starting to extort them, and I'd never heard of them before."

"There can't be too many of them, then," she concluded, "otherwise they wouldn't agree to pay. Can't be too few of them either, or the horcs would have just killed them."

"My thoughts exactly."

"I'll call Abigail and give her the information. Your turn to watch," she said, handing me the binoculars. She rooted around again for the communicator and raised Abigail. From the sound of it, Abigail hadn't heard of any mushroom people, either. Chalk up another discovery to the power of spying.

"You go ahead and get some rest. I'll keep watch until I'm tired and then wake you," I said once she ended the conversation. She didn't object and settled onto her mossy bedding platform, holding one of her swords in her hand. A few minutes later, I heard her breathing even out into the slow shallowness of sleep.

The night passed quickly, and I woke up Diana after three hours of sleep, informing her to wake me up at dawn. Morning comes early in the summer this far north. Before I knew it, she was nudging me awake. It felt like I hadn't slept a wink, but the rosy eastern sky reflecting off her green-scaled skin said otherwise.

"Wanna bite?" she asked, holding up a slice of pemmican wrapped in linen.

I sat up and took the food. "Thanks. Anything?"

She shook her head. "Only a few night creatures. No horcs, rat men, or vulture men."

I grunted through my mouthful of pemmican. It was definitely an acquired taste that I eventually became accustomed to. It took several tries—equal parts pounded dried meat and melted fat wrapped in linen is both greasy and dry at the same time. However, it traveled well, kept damn near forever, packed a high caloric punch, and tasted better than famine tubes. Although most of his cooking was geared for sustenance over flavor, Gormond whipped up a mean batch of pemmican; he even included berries when they were in season.

As I finished my breakfast, a thought occurred to me. "Diana, have you ever seen a cookbook?" I asked.

"No. What is it?"

"It's a book containing information on how to cook food."

She snorted. "It's not hard to cook food. Put it into the fire until you can eat it. If that doesn't work, put it in a pot of boiling water and wait until you can," she responded simply.

"Cookbooks contain ingredient lists and specific directions on how to heat the food," I said.

She gave me an uninterested shrug.

"If you ever find one, I'll give you two gold eagles for it." That got her attention.

"How would I recognize one?" she inquired, eyes narrowing.

"If you find a book with a lot of pictures of food, you've probably found a cookbook."

"It's a deal." She held out her hand and I shook it. "I'm going to hold you to this, Stonewall. You're not going to weasel out of this one." She took a swig from her canteen to wash down breakfast.

"If you could give me a few minutes," I said, changing the subject, "I want to listen to the recordings of the past few hours."

She nodded. "I'll keep watch."

I ran through the recordings and hit pay dirt less than ten minutes in—a conversation setting up the assault against the rat men.

"Bingo! They're coming tomorrow at noon," I told Diana as she clicked on the communicator to reach Abigail. "It'll be easy to have everything in place by then." Smart—the vulture men were attacking when the rat men would be least active and have the fewest guards or scouts outside, if any at all.

Abigail was pleased to hear the news and let us know she'd get the ball rolling. Three squads of ten warriors armed with rifles would march out of Deeplac long before sunrise tomorrow. They would arrive in that mid-morning sweet spot:

an hour after the rat men head back into their nest and two hours before the horcs were supposed to attack.

"Well," I said to Diana as I clicked off the communicator, "We've got nothing to do except wait."

She nodded and leaned back against one of the barricade pillars. "Could be worse." She lifted an arm and pointed toward the east. "Just look at that sunrise." Her green sales flickered with a soft hint of opalescence in the early rays. We watched the sunrise in silence for a few minutes before hiding behind a pillar, waiting for the sun to cease illuminating our mossy observation point.

"So this power source..." she said suddenly, as if we'd been talking about it. "It has to be underground, doesn't it? If the rat men didn't know what it was, it couldn't have been in the aboveground part of the mall. The rat men had to have gone over every inch of their home over the generations, if out of nothing but boredom. You try keeping the kids from exploring," she added to strengthen her case, like I was arguing against her. "It has to be underground, somewhere behind a big metal door or behind a collapse."

"That's my take on it," I concurred. "The rat men constructed the mound over the mall, so they'd already explored all they could before they started dragging trash over it."

"When we get in there, we've got to throw that egg around and see what it shows up. Tell it to go into every nook and cranny it can find. If there's a collapse, perhaps there's a way it can get through and then we could figure out how to dig the power source up from a different direction."

"I think we could talk Abigail into allowing it," I said, surprised that she was so interested in the power source.

"Because if we could find it and move it," she said animatedly, "we could have power in Deeplac. Just think what Marylyn and Elissa could do with constant, reliable power!"

I nodded. "I'm of the same opinion. If we could get power in Deeplac, Marilyn's already stated she could move the food machine. We'd be able to feed another thirty or so sentients a day, easy."

She leaned her head back, considering a future Deeplac, powered and filled with the scents of haggis, mince pie, and Cullen skink. "It would be nice," she said wistfully.

"If you think that's nice, you'd love air conditioning."

"Air conditioning?"

"It's a machine that blows out cool air, allowing you to turn the hot days of summer into spring-like temperatures. At least for indoor areas."

Her eyes widened at the thought. "I've got a new goal in life then!" She laughed and raised her sword. "I pledge to find air conditioning!" she mockingly announced.

Sitting on a clump of moss in the middle of a ruined I-94, the skeletons of my old civilization collapsed around me in all directions, I lifted my knife and pledged with her.

Chapter Eleven

Mystify, Mislead, and Surprise

Although we had intel that the attack wasn't until tomorrow, we went about our surveillance as normal. We took turns on watch facing east, kept an eye out on the rat men facing west, and stayed vigilant just in case the Hayden Miles Dannavant's plans changed. One of the primary rules of my business is never trust what someone else says, or to put it more accurately with the old Russian quote: "Doveryai, no proveryai." Trust, but verify.

We each took a nap during the late afternoon, doubling up on our rest for the day and reducing the chance of our falling asleep during night watch. I also checked on the recordings at nearly real-time to reduce the chance of being surprised if the Dannavant decided to move up the timetable of his raid.

All of our precautions proved unnecessary, as the day and night passed without incident. When I woke, the bug confirmed the vulture men's raid was still on schedule. Additionally, I learned that there were forty-five horcs involved in the raid, split into three squads in order to attack each of the entrances. The assault would begin at the southern entrance, intensify via the hidden entrance five minutes later, and then climax with a breach of the northern entrance. The Dannavant hoped to roll up the rat men from behind.

I contacted the Deeplacers, who were already on their way, updating them on the battle plans should they need to adjust their own forces and tactics accordingly. Diana and I had a couple of hours before the horcs arrived, so we readied ourselves. We cleaned our rifles—sequentially, obviously— and double-checked our other gear. Between us, we had one hundred rounds of ammunition.

Naturally, a few vulture men would act as commanders for the raid, but Abigail doubted they would actually enter the mall during the attack. Apparently, the vulture men had a shared fear of underground spaces and never willingly entered subterranean areas. These commanders would be perched outside the mound with a clear view of Deeplac's troops, armed with rifles, entering the fray to fight the victors amongst the horcs' and rat men's conflict. Such information would likely stir immediate action—a flight back to the Lancaster Building to inform the other vulture men of our attack and our unexpected weapons upgrade.

That's where Diana and I came in; our task was to take out any vulture men once the warriors of Deeplac initiated combat. The plan was to kill them all to prevent knowledge of the Deeplacers' strike; the longer the vulture men remained ignorant of our rifles, the better it was for us. Even if we were made, we could take out a few vulture men along the way and we all agreed that the world could use a few less vulture men.

We kept watch until five vulture men flew out of the Lancaster Building, at which point we retreated to the center of I-94 and hid behind one of the pillars to remain out of sight. The sound of talons against plascrete broke the silence, announcing the vulture men's landing on the upper deck, facing the rats' nest. Upon that signal, we sidled our way back to our observation post, waiting for visual confirmation of the horc advance.

It took fifteen minutes for the horcs to come into view. They marched in three columns, and a quick count showed forty-eight instead of the expected forty-five; the vulture men must not have included the squad leaders in their total. The horc at the head of the center column—the one I pegged as the platoon leader—carried an unusual metal contraption on his shoulders. Worn like a reverse backpack, a short, wide barrel protruded from its center. I didn't recognize it, but I had no doubt it was a weapon of some sort, perhaps some sort of siege machine or a futuristic portable door breacher. Whatever it was, it was big; I wouldn't be able to wear it. It would take someone like Reginald or Grendel to use it.

I admit it—I was already divvying up the treasure. I've always been a fan of new gear.

We ducked behind the barricade once the horcs were close enough to spot us and waited for them to pass. As they marched under the bridge, we silently migrated to the western edge of I-94, only a dozen or so feet beneath the vulture-men commanders. The din of marching troops covered our movement, and the nanobots scrubbed our scent from the vulture men's keen sense of smell.

Given the size of the rat men's mound, we couldn't see the southern or northern entrances, but the hidden entrance was easily visible, as were the squad of horcs climbing the mound toward it. They stopped about fifty yards out, waiting as we were for the sounds of combat from the southern entrance.

It didn't take long; a few minutes passed, then battle cries heralded the horc's assault on the southern entrance. Their ploy was simple—the captive rat man would convince the guards at the southern gate to let him in, and then the horcs would attack once the gates were opened. Given the lack of gunfire or continued shooting, I had to guess the invading forces succeeded in their surprise.

A little less than five minutes later, the horcs on the eastern entrance sprang into action, quickly crawling over the mound until they reached the hidden gate. They dealt with the gate in a remarkably primitive fashion: standing upon it and jumping up and down until the bar broke from the stress. As each horc was at least 350 pounds and there six jumpers, it was no surprise the gate couldn't take the punishment. The horcs fell down into the sloping entrance and the sound of gunshots indicated a decent rat-man defense. I saw two horcs take a round before they silenced the shooter. One of the horcs was killed, the other only wounded.

A few minutes after the assault on the hidden gate, a loud sizzling thwump announced the northern assault. It was followed by a small cloud of smoke rising over the mound from the north entrance that drifted slowly westward. I rued the fact that I wasn't able to witness the gate-breaker in action, as the evidence of its use was impressive.

As the horcs did their—and our—dirty work, only rare snippets of combat reverberated this far from the mall. Once all the vulture men's ground troops were inside, we allotted them thirty minutes of fighting before beginning our assault. There wasn't anything for us to do beside wait for our moment to act. To borrow an old but familiar adage, battle is months of boredom punctuated by moments of terror. While in this case it was hours, rather than months, the feeling held true.

Our plan was a duplicate of the horcs', which led me to think that somewhere among the vulture men, there was a sound tactical mind. We'd start at the southern entrance, then go through the hidden entrance, and once all opponents were facing south against our influx, attack from the rear via the northern entrance. Abigail headed the northern group, where we anticipated the strongest resistance, and our best shots were with that contingent, but we'd incorporated at least three good shots in each of the other two groups amidst the lesser shots.

Once inside, the squads would split with one half ascending

to the second level, and then divide again to cover each wing of the mall. This covered the greatest amount of area while also providing concentrated fire throughout the main hall. It would also force the defenders to split their troops or face being flanked or encircled.

The time ticked by and eventually the Deeplacers moved from their concealed positions. Like us, the vulture men sitting on the barricade twenty feet above us couldn't see the northern or southern entrances, but they had eyes on the eastern. Diana and I remained absolutely quiet beneath them while the Deeplacers broke cover to advance on the hidden entrance, watchful for the vulture men's response. They hadn't spoken much up until then, but the arrival of unexpected interlopers elicited much distress.

"What's this?! Who? I don't recognize them," the Hayden Miles Dannavant spluttered quietly, not wanting to alert the unknown troops on the ground of their location. I had listened to their conversations for so long, I could identify many of them by voice.

"I don't know. What are they doing here?" an unknown vulture man said.

"How did they know? Did they follow us?" the Aldrich Yates Whitaker IV, a board member, questioned.

"Quiet!" the Dannavant cautioned. "Watch!"

"They all have rifles! Where did they get so many rifles?" the unknown vulture man interjected, and the Dannavant breathily hissed for him to shut up.

The Deeplacers crawled over the trash of the mound, pausing just prior to the entrance to gather their forces and approach with three rifles abreast. They peered over the entrance, and seeing nothing, proceeded into the depths of the mall.

"We must warn them!" the Hayden Miles Dannavant commanded. "Fly to the northern entrance and shout down the hole; the horcs should be able to hear you. Now, go now!"

A vulture man took flight, dropping down beneath the upper deck of I-94 before catching enough wind to rise toward the north. Luckily he didn't see us, having jumped from the opposite side of the massive support pillar we were against. He quickly flew across the mound and was greeted by gunfire— four shots rang out and one hit his left leg. The injured vulture man cried out, banked hard, and headed back toward the highway.

I lowered my binoculars; Diana and I were done waiting. I leaned over to her and whispered, "I'm going to the other side. You take out the injured one coming back and that should flush them out toward me."

She nodded and I moved as quickly and quietly as I could across the lower deck, thanking the climate for the masses of moss that made it easier than it could have been. The east side gave me the longest field of view to target the retreating vulture men and I had five shots in my rifle's magazine. I was just past the halfway point when Diana's rifle rang out, and quickly looking backward, I caught the glimpse of a dead vulture man falling from the sky about fifty yards away from the highway.

The noise of her shot startled the vulture men above, and they scattered in a cacophony of flapping wings that I could hear even this far away. Abandoning stealth, I sprinted toward the eastern side, rifle ready to prevent them from notifying the main body of vulture men. The first one was dead before he flew ten yards into my field of vision. The second was dead at thirty. The third I grazed with the first shot but killed with the second. The fourth, figuring out my location, dove down behind the rooftops of the ruins, using them as cover. I almost got him when he popped his head out to look at me, but I missed by an inch. Of course, the one I failed to kill was the Hayden Miles Dannavant. That's my luck, sometimes.

His big black dead eyes spotted me while I reloaded. We had previous dealings and judging by the look on his face, he remembered me. That was unfortunate, but not without a contingency plan. I pulled the rifle and scope up just in time to watch the Dannavant disappear into the Waukegan skyline.

"Did you get them?" Diana asked, arriving a second later.

"All but one of them, dammit."

"So are we blown?"

"We're blown. They know it's Deeplac. It was the Dannavant that got away."

She retrieved the communicator from my backpack and

hailed Abigail. There was a quick exchange of information before hanging up.

"Abigail will get a ride from Brum and be in Deeplac in an hour, in case the vulture men get feisty and decide to attack while our forces are away."

"How's it going inside?"

"She thinks all the rat men are gone. A few of the horcs are dug in like a tick and we can't break through. But it's just a matter of time; they don't have food or water."

I nodded. "Orders for us?"

"She wants us to join the northern entrance team inside. Also, you're supposed to stay on top of the recordings. I'm supposed to go in and break up the horcs."

I raised an eyebrow.

"They're using bladed weapons." She grinned.

"Well…it's just a matter of a short time, then," I said with a grim smile.

We descended from I-94 and met the guard stationed at the northern entrance half an hour later. During the trip, I listened to the live feed of the vulture men to keep on top of anything they might plan. So far I had nothing, but they could just as easily be talking in another room and I'd never know.

The guard waved us in and daylight disappeared as we traveled the long tunnel to the north part of the mall. We clicked on our flashlights as we passed several rat men and horc bodies before the tunnel opened into the main corridor of the mall. Most of the fighting must have occurred in the courtyard; dozens of corpses—both rat men and horcs—littered the area into which we debouched. A single floor lamp with three red bulbs illuminated the space.

"Diana!" Drat waved at us from the entrance of what was once the anchor store of the north wing. "You're needed over here!" We followed him into the store, stepping over remains as we went.

"There are more rat men than I thought," I said to Diana.

"They must have gotten some reinforcements from the splinter communities." She shook her head indifferently. "Or there might have always been more than we knew about."

"The horcs really tore them up. I was certain they had more firearms, but it looks like they only had a few, or limited ammunition. I wonder, where is the silvery pistol that Conner had?" Conner was the rat man who usurped power from the previous ruler and abducted Marilyn. I wouldn't miss him.

"We got it," Drat said. "Abigail took it and handed it over to Marilyn. She didn't know what it did, and if Conner used it, you can't tell from the wounds on the dead. None of them look like anything special. Marilyn's going to wait till she gets it back to Deeplac to mess around with it."

Well that was interesting—a weapon that Marilyn couldn't identify? "What about the cannon-thing the leader horc was wearing?"

"We've got that, too, and it's also with Marilyn," he

responded. "However, you'll need to grow a little if you ever want to use it." He chuckled.

He led us up an employee-only stairwell illuminated by a single dim red bulb. We passed a storage area that was being picked over by a crew of three of ours before we turned to the left. He stopped and pointed down a long hall, also illuminated by a single red bulb. "All the way down the hall, last door on the right. That's where the last of the horcs are holed up."

Beyond several dead horcs and in front of the target door were two dead Deeplacers, the first I'd seen. "We take any more casualties?"

"No, just Wil and Cor. They said they had a plan." Drat sighed wistfully. "It wasn't a good one."

"They were always risk takers," I noted. "Bound to catch up with them eventually."

He nodded and addressed Diana, "Time to do your thing."

She drew out one of her swords and slowly walked down the hall, carefully avoiding as much blood as possible. As she went, she whistled a flat tune, informing the horcs of her impending arrival. No sense surprising them when you want them readied with their bladed weapons. How were they to know that any blade used against the Blade Witch would only damage its wielder?

It was a short fight, if "fight" was even the right word. I don't think Diana actually bloodied her weapon; the horcs managed to slay themselves for her. She walked out in less than fifteen seconds.

"They're dead," she announced, sliding her sword into its scabbard.

"Good. Let the looting commence!" Drat exclaimed, taking quick leave to start; he looked a little annoyed that he'd been prevented from starting earlier.

I called out to Diana, who stood near the far door, "Want to find Marilyn with me or do you want to loot?"

"I'm going to loot for a while," she replied, following Drat's lead.

"All right then, it was a pleasure working with you again."

"Likewise," she said, turning back into the room she'd just left.

I went downstairs and asked the crew in the storage room where I could find Marilyn. They told me she was in the food court, so I left the anchor store and headed south. As I went, I passed clusters of bodies, each a place where a group took a stand and died, or died together seeking a more defensible position. The food court wasn't far away and it was also illuminated by a single floor lamp with three red bulbs. I wondered where they got the bulbs. Did they have a stash of them or did they find normal bulbs and then paint them red?

I rounded the corner and found Marilyn, Broagh, and Reginald huddled around a large machine behind the counter of a garishly decorated store. Although many of the decorations were lost or torn, large swatches of various plaids that matched what could only be called vomit-green walls encircled the entire edifice. A dark neon sign hung proudly: "MacDonall's." That piqued my interest. I loaded up the interior information I had for the Gurnee Mills Mall in my memory storage and none of the twelve different floor plans I had indicated that the eatery had ever existed. It must be from my future.

"Heya, Marilyn!" I called out as I approached.

She turned around and waved jauntily. "Ah! Stonewall, just the person I wanted to see! Come around here and give us some help."

I slid over the counter. "What do you need?"

"I want you to cut these bolts out of the floor with your plasma cutter. No matter what tool I use, I can't get any grip; they're all stripped and gutted."

"No problem." I lit up the plasma cutter and cut cone-shaped exclusions around the four bolts that she'd indicated. The food machine, labeled "Dempster 3000" was a large plaid-colored box about the size of a double-conveyer pizza oven. It probably weighed a ton, but there looked to be a convenient join in the middle that would separate it into two smaller pieces for shipping. Not that a thousand-pound hunk of metal was going to easy to move, but it's a lot easier than a two-thousand-pound one.

"How's that?" I asked after cutting out the last bolt.

Broagh pushed on the machine and it moved. *Looks like it worked*, he broadcast.

Marilyn checked it over and agreed. "I should have it disassembled in an hour. Brum should be back by then to take one of the pieces, and we'll assemble a team to pull the other one."

"I'll take a first round on the pull team," I ventured. "Getting the load out the door and down the mound will be the hardest part."

I'll be working with you, as will Grendel, Broagh said. *Between us, we should be able to move it along quickly.*

"Stonewall, did you get any of the mince pies?" Marilyn asked, moving toward a bag resting on the counter.

"No, but I'd love to tear into a few!" Gormond's pemmican was good, but not that good.

She pulled three little hand pies out of the bag and passed them my way. "We're going to save the rest for the sentients back home. A little something special," she said with a smile.

I wolfed down two of the pies in almost as many seconds. "Ah…sooo good," I managed to say before the third one disappeared as well. "These are going to be a big hit if we can get the machine to work."

"I'm hoping I'll be able to. It may take a while, and I may need the power source located here, although some in the council aren't keen on the idea."

They'll come around if you can show the benefits outweigh the negatives, which I think you'll be able to do, Broagh said with a friendly pat on Marilyn's shoulder. *A few more pies wouldn't hurt.*

"Speaking of power, do either of you have the silvery egg? Diana had the idea to run it around the mall, looking for nooks and crannies leading to a basement level," I asked, licking the grease from the last pie off my fingers.

"As a matter of fact, I have it right here," Marilyn said, removing the egg from one of her belt pouches. "You've got at least an hour of scanning time before we have to head out. If you can find the power source by then, we may be able to postpone the move if we can get to the power source and remove it with a few hours of work."

I took the egg. "I've got an idea where it might be located. Let me check that out first. If I find anything, I'll find you."

Marilyn turned the unbolted Dempster back on, fed it some broken wood, and made a few more pies before dissembling the food machine. "We'll be here."

Chapter Twelve

Batteries Not Included?

Map in head and flashlight in hand, I headed toward the maintenance and services area. It was underground and on the west end of the mall, accessible via staircase or elevator. I tried the elevator first but found it crushed and filled with debris. The stairs beside the elevator also seemed impassable. To be thorough, I popped up the egg with instructions to find a way through either if it detected one. It did not.

Since my first hunch didn't pan out, I had to do it the hard way; sending the egg out for a full multi-level search, which I expected to take half an hour or more. With careful instructions to travel wherever it could squeeze, and to not consider an area closed until the egg was within two inches of a wall, I let it go.

With nothing to do for the foreseeable future, I sat on a broken piece of concrete and turned off my flashlight. First rule beneath the shattered moon: don't waste power. Okay, that's not really the first rule, but no one listens to what you're saying if you call it rule thirty-eight or rule forty-one, so I've got a lot of "first rules."

It took a while for my eyes to adjust to the dark, and the

dim red glow of faraway lightbulbs was once again the only source of illumination. If we could find this power source, the future of Deeplac could radically change. Electricity wouldn't just provide lighting and heating, it could also be used to power tools, the bellows on the furnace for the blacksmith—if not the furnace itself—and water pumps that could eventually lead to running water and internal plumbing. If Marilyn could jury-rig some sort of electric-powered tractor or tiller, machine power could boost food production which could precipitate a population boom, or at very least ensure that we could support our growing number of refugees, which, frankly, would be a very good thing given how life in Deeplac was leaps and bounds better than what I've heard about in other places. There was a reason the population had doubled in the past four months.

The community's success was largely predicated upon Abigail; her secret ability to read minds was the reason that the psychos and murder-hobos which plagued other lands had been absent from Deeplac since its founding twenty-odd years ago. The larger and faster the village grew, the more risk there was of disrupting its social cohesion, and Abigail wasn't going to be around forever. Sure, there were ways to extend one's lifespan—a dose of AeternrX could give her another ten years on average if I bucked the odds and found a dose and she tolerated it, but any longer than that would require technology beyond my time. I'm not even sure I would recognize it even if I ever saw it. The safer bet was to set up a system that could function without her—unlikely, considering how well things have gone under her leadership.

The egg returned while I was deep into musing about possible futures. I turned on its holographic map and it lit up the surrounding ruins in a shifting green light. The newly discovered lower level immediately caught my eye, and I zoomed in, hoping to find power lines that I could trace back to a main system, but there were no traces. I knew they had to be there, so I tightened in the map and carefully looked at the entire lower level. I found plenty of plumbing and HVAC lines, but nothing I recognized as exposed wiring.

I clicked off the map and walked back to the food court. Broagh and Marilyn were neck-deep in separating the food machine into transportable sections.

"The egg found a lower level, but I can't make heads or tails of it," I announced as I arrived.

Marilyn absorbed the tool she had in her hand. "Let's take a look then."

I summoned the map and focused on the lower level. "I see a whole bunch of plumbing lines, but I can't find a single power line," I complained.

Marilyn squinted at the map, and pulled it to the left and right until she zeroed in on a lump of machinery that looked like part of an HVAC system. It wasn't an overly large piece, perhaps three feet in both length and width, and roughly the same in height.

"We've got to find a way down there and we've got to retrieve that machine," she said empathetically. "We're not leaving without it."

"What?"

"Get out your plasma cutter," she ordered. Baffled, I pulled it out of my bag. She pulled me over by the arm to the three-bulb floor lamp. "Now cut that out—a wide circle around the whole unit." I looked to Broagh, who was just as puzzled as I was, but he didn't need to tell me it was best to obey Marilyn when she spoke in such a tone.

I made one quick circular turn of the wrist, severing the standing lamp from its base. Remarkably, the globes remained lit. The tinker bent down, prying her black paws under the unit without much success. "Help me pull this up," Marilyn said. "It's too heavy for me.

Broagh and I went to the post, lifted it out of the floor, and laid it across two broken benches. The lights didn't even flicker.

"What? Where are the wires?" I asked, examining the single circular metal canister at the liberated base.

Marilyn smiled and pointed back to the egg's map floating near the counter of MacDonall's. "That, my friend, is because there are no wires; it's a broadcast power station, and this," she said, tapping the circular half-dome underneath the lamp, "is a receiver tuned to its broadcast."

"So…wireless power?"

"Yep! Although it's got to be on a thin bandwidth or a small broadcast radius, otherwise anything requiring power nearby would be lit up. My guess would be both, but we'll be able to test that once we get it out of the basement."

"I'll study the map and figure that part out. There's got to be an easy way, and if there isn't, I get the feeling you're going to demand the hard way," I said, chuckling.

"You got the right feeling," she professed. "But having the power station is useless without the receivers. I'm going to need you to cut out as many of these as we can get." She nudged the metal dome for emphasis.

"I can't be two places at once," I protested. "Why don't you just take my plasma cutter and have someone else cut out the red lights in the mall? They are easy enough to spot and gather at the food court for transport."

The tip of her tail started to twitch nervously and Broagh's quills rose at my suggestion. Again with the sharing taboo? I took one on her paws in my hands. "Look, we share all the time, for the good of Deeplac, don't we?" I asked with enough vagueness just in case Broagh didn't know about the parabolic microphone.

Marilyn brushed the white streak of fur on her head with her other hand. "Those are communal goods that are being used communally, albeit by a specific individual," she replied nebulously. So she hadn't told Broagh. "This is your plasma cutter," she said emphatically.

I prepared myself for some mental gymnastics. "As

residents of Deeplac, we are all communal tools working for the betterment of the community, and our possessions are merely extensions of our innate abilities. You didn't worry when I used my strength to help lift the lamp; why should you worry when I allow you to use my cutter in pursuits for the improvement of Deeplac?" Both council members chewed on that for a bit. "Plus, you need me to find a way to that power source. Not to brag, but no one else can do that as well as I can. It would be a waste of my skills—as a communal resource—to have me go around the mall and cut out lamps."

They looked at each other and had a conversation of glances before Marilyn nodded. "William, I'm going to keep your cutter for a while, but I promise to return it once we are done collecting receivers." She turned to Broagh. "Dear, I need you to tell everyone to stop what they're doing and come to the food court. We've got to form a team to loot all the power receivers in the mall, functioning or non-functioning."

As I examined the map more closely, Broagh nodded and sent out a powerful blast, summoning everyone to the food court within fifteen minutes. Marilyn passed the cutter off to Reginald, whose height and strength made him a good retrieval man. His youth made him too uncomfortable to not accept an elder councilor's assignment, taboo or not, and he accepted the extraction team of six she formed around him with equal aplomb. Everyone else was sent off to locate as many receivers as they could find; each sentient given an area to cover with preference for functional over broken units. Everyone was to report back within the hour with their information.

By the time the orders were given and the crowd dispersed, I thought I'd found a way to the power source. There was a discrepancy between the final plan in my storage and the egg's map: a floor access panel was in my map but the egg's map had normal tiled flooring.

"I think I may have found a way down, but I don't have a pry bar so I can't test it until Reginald gets back with the plasma cutter," I told Marilyn and Broagh as they continued separating the food machine into parts.

Marilyn held out one hand, and the wad of gray goo that appeared there turned into a pry bar. "You can take one of mine," she said slowly and cautiously. "But be sure to return it." Sometimes I forget she's a walking toolbox; maybe this sharing thing could take off...

"Will do, chief," I responded as I started toward the suspect section of the mall. I turned on my flashlight and headed south. I got to the space indicated on my building plans and had to move a horc body out of the way. Positioning my light to illuminate as much flooring as possible, I gave the floor a hearty bang with the sharp end of the bar, testing every twenty feet in each direction to detect the section with a different reverberation. The thuds were eventually met with a ping—jackpot!

I started breaking and prying away the tile over that section of flooring, and it didn't take long to reveal a pair of thick metal doors underneath the tile. I hacked away for another ten minutes, clearing the doors of the tile, concrete, and grout before prying the bar between them. They didn't budge—likely locked or barred on the other side. Neither would stand in the way of my plasma cutter, but there wasn't much I could do until Reginald finished with it, so I went to the food court and returned Marilyn's pry bar.

She absorbed the heavy metal rod into her extended hand and breathed a sigh of relief before quietly swearing at her hulking nemesis: a fully intact Dempster 3000. I had a moment of inspiration.

"Did you bring those gloves you made that can lift metal objects?"

"Yes," Marilyn said, between mini grunts as she strained with a bolt.

"Couldn't you just use them on this and we could walk out of here right now?"

She stopped working. "I could, but this is a functional piece of machinery. The gloves set up an anti-gravity field that relies upon the object's magnetic attraction, and I'm not sure what that's going to do to live circuitry. I need to test it out on something relatively worthless. This," she said, tapping the food machine, "is far from worthless."

"That it is," I agreed. "I'm going to hang out here until Reginald gets back with the plasma cutter. Anything I can do while I'm here?"

"Sure, you can start with this blasted bolt," she said, faux-kicking its side. Broagh let out one of his toothy smiles, but was wise enough not to chitter.

"All right, I'm all yours," I said with a similar smile and prudent lack of laughter.

I spent the next half hour taking commands from Marilyn. You'd think that breaking down a machine for transit would be a simple affair, but the makers of the Dempster 3000 obviously intended it to remain intact in one place once assembled. Inner connections were intentionally placed to make it difficult to undo, which added stability to the structure with moving parts, but was terribly frustrating when you were carefully trying to deconstruct it for later reassembly.

During the process, sentients started drifting back into the food court after exploring their areas for receivers. By the time we finished, we were all waiting for Reginald to return. He strode in after a few minutes, carrying more than two dozen power receivers, eleven of which functioned. Before he could start reporting in full, I asked for my plasma cutter and made my exit, along with Broagh. Marilyn could figure out how best to loot everything without us; we were on a different mission. If the power source was there as the map said, it would become our primary objective and everything else would have to wait.

I lit up the plasma cutter as soon as I got back to the metal doors. First, I slit down the center, assuming I'd cut through a bar of some sort, but the doors remained sealed. Then, I went after the hinges. Slicing the third hinge of one side did the trick, and the door collapsed inward with a large crash.

I laughed like a kid opening a Christmas present and Broagh looked at me, askance. I shrugged my shoulders and fired a big grin. "I can't help it, I just love going where I'm not supposed to."

That does explain a lot, Broagh commented.

"Why yes, yes it does." I beamed. My snarky pincushion of a companion couldn't dampen my enthusiasm. I lit the newly created hole with my flashlight, passing it throughout the entire area.

"This used to be the end of the mall when it was first built and this was an elevator shaft. To our good fortune, it looks like they decided covering it was easier than filling it in," I assessed while taking rope out of my pack and tying it to the concrete stump of an old bench. Using my full strength, I pulled on the rope, testing to see if would hold my weight on the way back up. It held, so I went to the edge and then over and down.

"You coming?" I asked, hanging a few feet beneath the floor.

I'm going to head back to the food court and see if Marilyn's ready to go exploring for the power supply. I'll pick up Diana as well and join you in about five minutes, he said. *Don't go too far.*

"I won't," I assured him, sliding down the rope to the basement floor twenty feet below. About an inch of water covered the floor. "Broagh!" I yelled.

His face poked over the edge. *Yes?*

"Could you pass me something I can poke the ground with? There's water down here covering the entire floor and I don't want to step in a hole."

Back in a second, he said before disappearing. He returned a minute later with the remains of a bench slat. *This should do*, he added before dropping it down, and left before I could respond.

I retrieved the slat and pressed it against the ground around me, ensuring there were no hidden holes. I hated walking in a thin layer of water; it gave you the vain illusion of safety. I'd rather walk in waist-deep water—there's fewer ways of hurting yourself in deeper water.

The shaft was at the end of a tunnel running north under the mall. I slowly made my way, prodding before each step until I came to a right turn in the hallway. I peeped around the corner and my light reflected off something round about a foot off the ground. I dropped the slat and drew my M1B, pointing at the reflection. I'm a cautious guy.

It didn't move, so I chanced it and tightened the beam of my flashlight for greater distance. That did the trick and I could see a full-sized crocodile lying about fifty yards in front of me. It must have been asleep, because its other eye opened at the noise of the slat and it started moving toward me.

I had no choice but to kill it with my blaster. I now had

sixty-three shots left. I felt a bit bad, but at least its carcass would be put to good use once we dragged it out of here and back to Deeplac. Imagine what Gormond could do with crocodile meat! But dinner was the least of my worries now; I had assumed this entire area was cut off from everything on the surface, but there had to be access somewhere. The croc was eating something, and judging by its size, the food supply couldn't be that unreliable. Perhaps more bothersome was the question of how a crocodile managed to survive underground in what was once Northern Illinois. It should be way too cold for them here, but if there was one, there's probably more.

I became acutely aware that I was alone and picked up the slat, making my way back to the hole and the rope. I called out but no one answered. I climbed up and started breaking down the bench Broagh had used into three more slats so everyone would have one when we went back down.

Broagh, Marilyn, and Diana arrived while I was trimming the slats with the plasma cutter. "There was a crocodile down there. I killed it," I announced.

"Crocodile?" Diana asked.

"It's an aquatic lizard almost twice as long as I'm tall."

She whistled at the size. "Never heard of them."

"That's because they shouldn't be here; they're warm-water creatures. They can't live in these temperatures."

Got to be something warm down there then, or they've decided they don't need warmth anymore, Broagh said.

It was a strange way to talk about mutation, but it was close enough. Perhaps they had mutated enough to deal with the relatively consistent temperatures below ground. "Either way, we need to be on guard," I said. "I'll take lead."

"How far is it to the power source," Marilyn asked.

"Not far—less than two hundred yards."

"All right, lead away."

I climbed down and the others followed, Broagh taking rear guard and Marilyn right behind me. We tapped our way to the corpse of the crocodile and it was met with appropriate oohs and ahhs.

"Huh—it's got the head of a crocophant on a giant lizard body," Diana noted. I broke into laughter and tears filled my eyes. Everyone stared at me.

"Sorry, passing bout of castaway sickness," I apologized once I collected myself.

Everyone nodded knowingly; these things were bound to happen occasionally when one was out of their time.

"This big guy is coming with us," I informed them. "You can eat them and their skin makes extremely tough leather."

Diana bent down and touched the row of scutes along its back and agreed, "It'd make some good armor."

"Let's move along," Marilyn urged. "We've got more important things to do." She was usually patient, but she was hot on the trail of a big find and didn't want to waste time poking a dead lizard, no matter how big it was.

We pushed our way past the croc and around another turn. Fifty feet further, the corridor opened up into a room lit by a single white bulb. We entered and the machine that drew her attention rested where the egg said it would be. Diana cautioned Marilyn back until I cleared the area, but she rushed to the power source nonetheless.

It wasn't much to look at, but it shared the same silvery metal casing that both the egg and Conner's gun possessed. The tinker hovered over it, assessing it from all angles without actually touching anything. Once she was certain of what she was doing, she took out a rag and wiped the thick layer of dust off its top. She rapidly examined the machine, pressing a multitude of buttons marked with symbols but conspicuously lacking labels. While she worked her mojo, the rest of us checked out the room and along the corridors, keeping watch for any danger. Thankfully, we didn't encounter any more crocs, but vigilance is its own reward.

After a half hour of fiddling, she finally spoke in her scholastic timbre, "Everything looks good. What we have here is a broadcast nuclear battery, and before you worry, there's no chain reaction going on, so we're completely safe. It's at about half charge, and I'd guess we have another two hundred years of power left drawing at full capacity. However, we won't be pulling anywhere near that power, so we've nothing to worry about: this thing will run long after our grandchildren's grandchildren are dead."

"That's a lot of mince pies." I smiled at our fortuity. "So, what do we need to do to move it?"

"Just pick it up and move it. It's not attached to anything. It's just a giant battery."

"But the thing weighs a ton," I protested.

"We'll figure something out," Marilyn replied pithily, letting us know there was no way she was leaving without this battery. "We'll need one of the sleds and we'll have to work out some impromptu rigging. So, let's get to work, shall we?"

Chapter Thirteen

Dark Skies

"Pick it up and move it" was easier said than done. Getting the broadcast battery down the tunnel wasn't that difficult once we'd gotten it on the sled, but lifting it out of the tunnel and into the mall proved to be a pain in the butt. It wasn't until I remembered we could use Marilyn's gloves to hold onto metal that a solution presented itself. I donned the oversized gloves, securing them with rope around my wrists so my hands couldn't slip out of them, and climbed along the support beam to the roof of the mall. Using my plasma cutter, I carved a small hole into the center of the beam, ensuring the edges were smooth. Threading it with thick rope, I created a fulcrum point, allowing us to hoist the battery out of the hole and push it to the side with our prodding slats.

The process took over an hour, a lot of muscle, and an equal amount of yelling. No doubt it would have gone faster had Arthur been around; he and his construction crew have had their fair share of logistical construction and demolition conundrums, and experience is the best teacher. Arthur and I don't see eye-to-eye on many things, but credit where it's due, he knows how to get things done quickly and efficiently.

Once the broadcast battery was in the mall and re-secured on a sled, things became much easier. We regrouped at the northern entrance and gathered up all of the loot we scrounged, sledding as many of the heavier objects as possible. In total, we had eight sleds worth of material, most of which was destined for Marilyn's workshop.

We only had a few hours of sunlight left by the time we exited the mall, and all of us had to take turns pulling the sleds to try to make the best time we could. As it was, we were cutting it close, and we might not arrive until after sunset. Since there was nothing else for me to do, I listened to the vulture men squabble while I towed my share of the weight.

And squabble they did There was a massive uproar about Deeplac, and the impassioned debate was punctuated by a cacophony of hisses, caws, and warbles. Although I was slowly picking up on some of the vulture men's unique language, it didn't take a linguist to understand what was happening; they were pissed and they wanted retribution.

I had periodically checked my bug throughout the early afternoon, but I had let a few hours lapse once we shifted focus on finding and liberating the battery from the mall. I expected a disproportionate amount of discussion to review and jumped to the more recent sections to get the most up-to-date information as quickly as possible, and then planned to work my way backward. The strategy paid immediate dividends, and I retrieved the communicator from my backpack.

Abigail answered and I informed her of the coming night raid. The news was less of a surprise and more of a confirmation of what we'd anticipated in our planning sessions. She had been back at Deeplac for hours, and by now all the immigrants should have moved out of their temporary housing and into the stronghold. They were getting integrated into Deeplac sooner than Abigail preferred, but it was the only way to ensure everyone's safety once the vulture men had made us on the battlefield. The stronghold didn't have anything to fear from the vulture men's dropped rocks—it was designed with that protection in mind. The other buildings could be damaged and possibly destroyed, but there wasn't much we could do about that except rebuild once the vulture men were no longer a threat.

I ended the communication and let Broagh know about the upcoming attack. He passed the word on to everyone and we picked up the pace. If we didn't make it back before nightfall, we risked not just our personal safety but having everything we'd scavenged destroyed by a stony hail. We kept a constant watch on the skies as we moved, and with significant effort, we made the gates of Deeplac within fifteen minutes of nightfall, just enough time to stash all the loot into the stronghold's communal sleeping room and to get my croc to the kitchen for skinning and butchering.

Once we were safely inside, Abigail ordered all the exterior light sources doused and limited the interior ones to those shielded from the outside. Vulture men have decent night vision, but it never hurts to make yourself harder to spot as a target. The residents of Deeplac knew the drill after the string of attacks from the wasteland raiders and helped the newer arrivals adjust accordingly. The newly acquired lights were a big hit with the kiddos, who immediately started playing in the ruby glow. Some were making shadow puppets while others opted to run and wave their arms and legs in front of the light, watching gleefully as their shadows moved on the wall.

We waited for about half an hour before the first taps of falling rock hit the roof of the stronghold. As the vulture men had done a few month earlier to the invaders at our walls, the rock rain came in waves, each composed of ten vulture men dropping roughly fifty pounds of rocks, each the size of a sling stone. I left the absolute safety of the internal rooms and moved to one of the exterior windows on the upper level that was out of the line of fire and sat down in the dark. Pauses of relative silence were peppered with bouts of torrential lithic precipitation. Much like a thunderstorm, the rhythmic beat on the roof was almost musical and pleasant to the ear, as long as you were safely inside.

As I waited and listened, Efte entered the doorway, her tiny form a darker shadow against the dimness behind her.

"Efte, you should go down to the communal room. It's dangerous to be up here," I warned her.

"I'm safe," she said in a no-nonsense tone. "It's you I'm

worried about."

I smiled. "You don't have to worry about me. I can take care of myself."

"That's not what they say," she stated emphatically

"They, as in the shadow people that follow me, they?"

Her darkened head nodded vigorously.

"Morien said I wasn't in danger from them."

"She's right, but she's also wrong. You're not in danger now, but you will be."

I raised my eyebrows but realized she couldn't see my face. "What do you mean?"

"You're going to take a trip soon," she started. Her shoulders rose as she continued. "They know you're going, even though you don't; they're going to get you killed on the way back." Her voice lowered, like she was telling me a secret, "They've talked to the Lawman and told him you're coming."

She finished with a deep breath and her shoulders relaxed. It was a long speech for an otherwise quiet kid. She stood completely still in the doorway, waiting.

"Do you know who the Lawman is?"

She shook her head no.

"I…I don't know what I should do, Efte," I replied. "What do you think I should do?"

She fumbled at her waist, drawing something out of her pocket. She walked over to me and commanded, "Put your arm out."

I complied and she wrapped something around my wrist three times, murmuring in the special language only she and Morien understood. She tied it off and explained, "This is a bracelet I made. When your spirits start to move something of yours, it will catch fire in a bright flash. I don't know if you'll have enough time to not die, but it's the best I can do."

I reached down and rubbed around my wrist; it was braided and thin. "What did you make this out of?"

"My hair—it's all I had." I found the thought of wearing a bracelet made of a little girl's hair to ward off angry spirits of people I had killed a little disturbing, but evened out my tone before speaking.

"How did you make this? Did Morien help?"

"I did it all by myself. While you were sleeping, I made some of your spirits flesh and claimed them as my own." A chill ran up and down my spine.

"You didn't wake me up?" I asked calmly but suggestively.

She shrugged. "I didn't think you wanted to wake up."

That checked—perfect kid logic. I took a knee and spoke to her eye-to-eye, "Next time you want to do that, you should wake me up. They are my spirits."

"I'm sorry! It's just that you have so many and—"

"It's okay, Efte," I said, holding my arms open to give her a hug. "I'm not mad, but you should always ask before you do things for someone, even if you're doing something nice. It's the polite thing to do."

She nestled against my chest. "Okay," she said softly. "I'll ask next time." I gave her a little affirmative squeeze before sending her off.

"Good girl. Now you should get out of here and go back to the communal room. Morien's probably looking for you already." I watched her shadow recede as she left the room and looked down at her gift. Did Morien know?

The vulture men were persistent with their attack, and they switched from attacking the stronghold to the outbuildings after two hours of ineffectually beating. The outbuildings couldn't take the strain, and the sound of their collapse echoed throughout the village. As projected, they were going to be a complete loss, but at least we'd have easy pickings for firewood this winter.

After three hours, tiredness took me and I went to my room and collapsed. I needed to speak with Morien tomorrow—I didn't know what was typical behavior for a young sorcerer, but I had the feeling this wasn't it…and I got the impression that Efte hadn't told Morien about any of this, either.

I hunted the elder sorcerer down at breakfast, but Efte was with her, so I went about my morning routine. Stepping outside, the early dawn sun revealed the complete destruction of the refugee barracks. Marilyn's old shack was on the other side of the stronghold, but if it was targeted in a similar manner, it too would have been destroyed. Arthur's crew was already at work, tearing up foundations and sawing the large logs down to firewood size. If they kept to form, they'd have it broken down before sunset.

Since there wasn't anyone needing medical evaluation, I took care of my mushrooms and brought the harvest to Gormond.

"Stonewall, would you teach me how to take care of your mushrooms?" he asked as I placed the basket on one of the kitchen tables. The crocodile corpse I left last night had already been pieced out and its hide sent for tanning.

"Are you muscling into my territory?" I teased.

He spluttered a bit, "No, I just thought I should know how, since you're occasionally gone for multiple days and everyone likes the mushrooms."

"I'm just kidding you," I reassured him. "I'll gladly teach you how to take care of them. They're pretty easy if you can do the first step right, which requires sterilizing the growth medium with boiling water." I grinned, "And, correct me if I'm wrong, but isn't boiling water your specialty?"

"That it is," he said, smiling in return, "that it is. When would be a good time for you?"

"How about sometime in the next few days? I have a few bags that are nearing the end of their productivity and need replacing soon."

"Just let me know when you're ready," he said, returning to his work.

I nodded and headed toward the roof of the stronghold. I

wanted to get a better look at the scope of the damage. Abigail and Grendel were there when I arrived, assessing the scene as well.

"Anything catastrophic?" I asked when I saw them.

"Nothing that can't be repaired," Grendel responded. "We're going to bring up more brick and layer it over the entire roof to absorb some of the shock."

Deeplac had large reserves of brick and wood, most of it underground in cellars. If there's one thing this strange post-apocalypse provides, it's brick and timber. Reclaiming building materials from past structures for current projects wasn't a new concept—like how the later Romans looted the grand structures of the Empire for their construction projects—only ruins regenerate under the shattered moon, making it more of a renewable resource.

"Anything I can do?" I offered.

"Was there anything new on the recordings?" Abigail inquired.

"Crap! I didn't check them this morning. I'll go do that now," I apologized.

Abigail and Grendel exchanged looks. "What's wrong? You never forget," she said.

I hesitated for a second—I should speak to Morien first, right?—but I acquiesced and told them about my encounter with Efte the night before. Abigail would find out eventually. They remained silent when I finished the story. "Thoughts?" I prompted.

Abigail hesitated before replying, "That's not how sorcery is supposed to work, I think."

Grendel agreed, "That's not the way I've always had it described to me."

"Should I speak with Morien? I tried this morning, but she was eating breakfast with Efte."

"We should probably speak with her together. She hates repeating herself," Abigail decided.

We found her outside watching Efte play with the other children. Morien arranged for someone else to mind her apprentice while we went to the council chamber for a private discussion. Once the door was closed, I relayed the previous night's conversation and showed her the bracelet.

She looked at it closely and sighed deeply.

"It's as I thought," she capitulated. "I have a big task ahead of me, a risky task."

"What do you mean?" Abigail asked.

"Efte is a reincarnate."

None of us said anything, waiting for her to explain.

"I've never explained how this works to you," she addressed Abigail and Grendel, "because there wasn't reason to do so, and it's closely guarded lore. But I can't bring this risk into your house without informing you of the full danger.

"Sorcerers hear the voices of the dead. We see their spirits, and they're constantly trying to gain our attention. Right now, there are...fourteen spirits talking to me and it takes focus and willpower to ignore them. That's one of the first things we teach our apprentices—they won't be able to harness their energy if they cannot find the silence within.

"From this silence, the prior masters speak to us, teaching us the magics they developed. Do you remember the spell I cast upon the hollow mummy?" she asked me. "The one that summoned the purple-black manacles?"

I nodded.

"That's Ariel's Bonds. It's one of the four spells Queen Ariel created. Her spirit taught it to me, and when I need to use it, I summon the silence within. In that silence, her spirit speaks to me once more and when I repeat her words, the magic happens. It's this way with all sorcerers. We use the magic of the prior masters as our own, and if we live long enough, if we're powerful enough, we create four spells that are uniquely ours that we pass on to other sorcerers when we're dead.

"In this way, we can achieve a sort of immortality. When I am dead, and I whisper one of my unique spells to other sorcerers and they use them, they send part of their souls to my spirit in exchange for my magic. Over time, when my spirit accumulates enough of a soul to reincarnate, I return, born into the body of a new infant. This is what Efte is. She is an ancient sorcerer reborn."

She paused to let us take in all of the information before continuing. From the looks on Grendel's and Abigail's faces, they were as out of their depth as I was.

"This is why Efte is dangerous—she isn't just herself, she's someone else as well…but I don't know who. I had an inkling that something was amiss when she identified a spirit I could not—"

"The blutgeist…" I interrupted.

She nodded. "I've been watching her carefully since, but now that she's made you that"—she pointed to my bracelet—"I know that she is a reincarnate. That level of magic is beyond me, beyond all but one of the sorcerers I have ever met. If we stay here, we put everyone in Deeplac at risk. Eventually, Efte will awaken to her full power and memory, and I don't know when that will happen or exactly who she'll be when it does. The safest thing to do is for us to leave and wander where there is less of a chance of anyone getting hurt." Her shoulders and head slumped forward in resignation.

"Do you have to raise her? Couldn't she just be exiled?" Grendel suggested.

"It's too late for that; she's bound to me as apprentice to master. As a reincarnate, were Efte to die, the ancient sorcerer would find a new child and find me again, and when she awakens, she'd definitely be angry with us." She looked down. "It's my fault. I wanted an apprentice so badly, I rushed into the connection even though I suspected the risk. I should have resisted the pull to pass on my knowledge." It was hard to see someone so normally staunch and unflappable surrender.

Abigail finally spoke, softly, and with an intimacy I'd never heard in her voice before, "Don't apologize for what you've done, Morien. Deeplac owes you a debt that far surpasses your single indiscretion. Whatever risk you have brought to us will be borne by all of us together. You are family and this is your home. Both you and Efte."

"We'll do what needs to be done," Grendel agreed.

Morien raised her damp eyes. "She's not just a danger, though. If she keeps a hold of herself and doesn't sublimate into the ancient sorcerer at her awakening, she'll be one of us. Her powers will be far greater than mine. If things go as we've planned, we'll benefit from her knowledge and ability."

"Is there anything we can do to help her succeed?" I asked.

"Be there for her when she asks. Answer questions. Make her feel safe. Attach her to this location and to the sentients around her. Make her feel wanted."

"We can do that," rumbled Grendel.

"I can't let her down now. So few people like me as it is, I gotta keep them close and happy," I joked. Everyone chuckled a little too readily; Abigail even let out a snort. I rubbed the thin bracelet on my wrist and wondered what consciousness lurked behind the eyes of the little girl I had rescued, and what would happen when it eventually came out.

Chapter Fourteen

This Is What It Sounds Like When Pigs Fly

With the mystery of my bracelet solved, Abigail unceremoniously kicked me out of the chamber and sent me to find Broagh to join them for "Elder Council Business." I found him with Marilyn and Elissa, neck deep in assembling the food machine, an impressive feat when you considering how many spines he has.

They had cleared the shelves and foodstuffs from the basement pantry of the kitchen to make room for the Dempster 3000—Marilyn and Gormond thought it best to keep the machine away from prying hands, which I agreed with wholeheartedly after inhaling the three mince pies put before me earlier. With everything moved to another nearby section of the basement, there was just enough space for the food machine, and the tinkers were busy reinstating the internal bolts that gave Marilyn such a hard time at disassembly. With Broagh's departure, I was tasked to hold everything in place while Marilyn made the last few attachments.

Elissa immediately picked up on my new accoutrement; sometimes I forgot that underneath that bubbly, perky personality was a keen, quick mind, a short-sighted bias on my part that Elissa was always correcting by being herself.

"Oh this?" I shook my elbow to move the bracelet on my arm without letting go of the metal box. "Efte made it for me." I opted to leave out the creepy parts.

"Looks like you finally made a friend," she teased, her ears twitched in her amusement.

"Eventually she'll get to know me and that'll end," I said self-deprecatingly.

"Don't be so hard on yourself, Stonewall; she'll probably stop liking you well before she gets to know you," Marilyn sassed back. "And we're done! Well, at least with that part. Let go slowly and see if the connection is secure."

I released my support gradually…no way was I taking the blame if this thing broke. The joints held and Marilyn seemed pleased with her work. She absorbed the wrench she had been using in one hand and formed a set of smaller fine-work tools in the other. "Now for the fun part…" she said with a delicious smile.

I chuckled. "I'll get out of your hair and leave you two to your work."

"I'm sure you'll be back just in time for the first pies that come out," Marilyn predicted.

"You know it!" I replied. With any luck, they would have the machine up and running by midday or dinner.

I made my way back to my chamber and fell upon my bed,

closing my eyes to better concentrate on the recordings I had failed to check that morning. There was a lot of material to get through, but after two hours, I was up to speed and out the door to track down Abigail.

"The vulture men are going to try something new tonight," I informed her. "They're going to drop large pieces of rubble instead of bags of gravel."

She quickly did some calculations in her head. "If they do as many runs as they did last night, that'll be what, nearly one hundred drops? How high are they flying on these drops? We need to find Arthur."

We found him amidst the rapidly reducing pile of debris that once was the refugee housing and informed him of the situation. Arthur looked down for a second, running the math in his head; the oversized armadillo had a gestalt with engineering. In the past, we often came to similar numbers, but I have several engineering degrees and a computer in my head—I don't know what fueled Arthur's acumen.

The plated elder shook his head and confirmed our misgivings. "That's going to be a lot of force on the stronghold; we are going to have to aggressively reinforce the roof." Arthur rounded up his construction team with new directives. "We need to start bracing the roof and eastern side of the stronghold, now."

Abigail added, "What if we convert the top level into a forest of braces and do the same with the exterior of the east side…that should be enough to last the night."

Arthur nodded with admiration. "You heard the lady. Let's get moving, we have until nightfall."

The crew dropped everything and all was a flurry of movement. Abigail nudged me out of the way. "Best to steer clear until he's done."

"I think we need to speed up our plan if they continue along this avenue of attack," I said. "I don't know how many days of continual beating the stronghold can take. It's not like they're going to run out of rubble to lift and drop our way."

Abigail shrugged. "I'm not overly concerned. We have always paid tribute and last night was the first time they had cause to attack. I think they are just testing our strength and resolve. But you should gather all your gear, just in case you need to move quickly."

"No harm being prudent," I agreed. We parted ways and I gathered my equipment, placing everything I'd need in the lockers that line the southern wall of my chamber. It took me a while to get used to having a row of gym lockers in my bedroom, but they're quite effective in keeping out nosy hands, especially when coupled with the three locks I'd scavenged with the locker bay.

Once that was settled, I poked my head into the basement to check on the food machine. Marilyn and Elissa had just finished their tinkering and were already cranking out the first batch of mince hand pies. I'd mistimed my arrival, however, and was third in line behind Grendel and Broagh.

Elissa gave me a hard time about being late and directed me upstairs, holding a pie in each of her hands. "Just in time to be useful! Go upstairs and get some platters—everyone is going to have a great lunch today!"

I spent the next half hour as an impromptu waiter, delivering hot pies to anyone who wanted one. There were progressively fewer sacks of mowed grass in the basement each time I went down for more pies, and the turnaround time was remarkably quick. You would load a bunch of clippings into the hopper and have fresh pies within seconds. If I didn't know better, I would have assumed it was some kind of magic—might as well be, Clarke's Third Law and such.

It was a joyous occasion and smiles broke out every time I came up from the basement with a platter of hot pies. I delivered a good twenty platters before Gormond and his crew took over. I found a seat in a corner and bit into the hot water crust, savory mincemeat in the middle and juice dribbling down my chin. If there were any naysayers on the nuclear battery at first, I doubted there would be after today. I sat back and watched everyone eat their fill. You get more than your fair share of bad times beneath the shattered moon, so who could blame me for wanting to stretch out a good one just a little longer. Plus, I needed to digest my pie.

Eventually everyone returned to the tasks of their normal day. I did the same, firing up the recordings of the vulture men to keep on top of recent developments. I was rewarded with a bunch of useless and vile chatter; it would be nice not to have to listen in on the odious creatures once we got everything sorted.

I spent the rest of the day pitching in with one of Arthur's construction squads, helping them break down all the destroyed temporary buildings and using what we could from that to brace the interior of the stronghold. I stopped every half hour to check on the bug and then return to moving heavy objects about. By the time the sun was on the way down, we'd managed to clear out all the refugee-related buildings, but Marilyn's old shack would have to wait until tomorrow. Given its diminutive size, it wouldn't take more than a few hours, but Abigail wanted everyone inside well before sunset.

I had dinner with Umma while the night trickled in. He was shoveling haggis into his maw at an impressive speed; I had never seen him happier.

"What are you going to do during the attack," I asked, making conversation.

"I was just going to stay down here," he said between mouthfuls of food, indicating the kitchen.

"I'll be along the eastern wall on the top floor, watching over one of the rooms, if you want to join me. If one of the braces breaks, it'd be easier if there were two of us to fix it."

"Sure, sure, I could do that," he accepted.

"I'm bringing my rifle and binoculars. I may be able to get

off a shot or two if things line up just perfectly."

He nodded. "I join you after a bit."

I headed up to the room I'd chosen to defend. The light was almost gone, so I removed the scope from my rifle and tried sighting with my binoculars. It went as well as you'd expect and I gave up on it after a few minutes of hassle—it simply wasn't going to work. I put the scope back on the rifle, picked up my binoculars, and spied the first wave of vulture men.

There were seven flying in a V formation, laboring under the weight of large pieces of rubble carried in slings. The slings were designed to allow the vulture men to fly while allowing the majority of the weight to rest on their shoulders. Secured with slip knots, the vulture men had only to pull the right piece of rope and the load would deploy. You couldn't say they weren't clever opponents.

My eyes were to the skies when Umma arrived. He'd forgone the crossbow he'd used for years after claiming a nice Glock 21 from the first dig. He wore it on a thin leather belt that looped around his portly figure and rested under his wings. It was the Glock that gave me the idea.

"Umma, I'm going to suggest something, and I want you to hear me out before you say no," I broached diplomatically.

"Okay," he grunted cautiously.

"I want to hire you for a mercenary job."

"What?" he sputtered.

"I need your special talents, and I'm willing to equip you

for the task and I'll pay you three gold eagles for one night's work."

That got his interest. "Okay, what's the job? What do you need?"

"I want you to fly out there and shoot all the vulture men you can with your pistol," I said calmly. "They're unarmed because they're carrying rocks. I don't see any vulture dogs with them, but that could change throughout the night, so that's a risk you'd have to take into consideration before you accept. I'll offer you two gold eagles to keep attacking until the vulture dogs arrive, if you'd rather not fight them."

"There's no way I'd be able to get them, Stonewall. It's too dark and I'd end up wasting all my ammo. I'll have to pass," he lamented as his shoulders slumped forward.

"Well, here's the thing," I said, patting my binoculars. "Since I'm hiring you to perform this mission for me, I'm responsible for equipping you so you can do it. If you think you could fly, hold these binoculars in one hand, and shoot your pistol with the other, we'd have a deal."

I could see him hesitate at such responsibility over someone else's private possession and quickly followed up with, "I'd tie the binoculars to you so there wouldn't be a chance you'd drop them."

Before he could respond, the first wave of rocks impacted the stronghold. Seven severe booms thundered against the building sending shudders through the flooring and walls. I looked out the window and watched the vulture men bank for the thirteen-mile trip back to their lair for more rubble.

"They're going to keep doing this all night. I need your services to break them up, for at least a few flights. If you manage to kill a few, that may be enough to break their will and they might call off the attack."

"Okay," he said. "I'll do it!"

"Atta boy!" I exclaimed with a strong clap on his shoulders. "You've probably got fifteen minutes or so before the next wave, so let's get you suited up and familiar with the binoculars so you can meet them before they enter Deeplac's air space."

We went up to the roof and I roped the binoculars to him and showed him how to use them.

"How much ammo you got on you?" I asked.

"I've got thirty rounds in three magazines," he responded.

I thought for a second. "Okay, here's what should work the best. The first wave you attack may tell the next wave that you're there, so you may only get one clean strike. However, even if they do that, they're not going to get back to their lair and bring their dogs with them until the third wave at the earliest, probably the fourth. This means you've got two waves for certain in which they won't be armed or guarded, and a potential third.

"On the first wave, get as close as you can to them before you fire and try to take two or three of them down. After that, land on the wall walk, catch your breath, and wait until you can see the next wave and start your attack from there. For the third wave, drop to the ground under some cover a few hundred yards outside Deeplac and then attack from there... they may not expect a salvo that far out, so you have a chance for another surprise attack. Come back to the stronghold after that one and we'll judge their response. You'll have earned two gold eagles just for that, and then you can decide if you want to continue."

He nodded and looked through the binoculars. "I see them. Got to go." He took a quick run and lifted his porky frame off the roof, little wings beating like mad. I retreated to the relative security of the room I was guarding and waited to hear gunshots.

The calm night was suddenly peppered by small arms fire, and two distinct screams that were undoubtedly vulturine. A few more rounds and another scream filled the night. There was a distinct lack of falling rocks, so Umma made good work on his first skirmish. The fifteen minutes before the next spurt of gunfire seemed to take forever, and the next wave had only two screams, but still, five injured vulture men might make them reconsider their tactics. Again, no impact on the roof despite the anticipation, and Umma had one more round to go.

The final wave was far enough away that the gunfire was barely audible, but I counted six shots. In total, Umma had used twenty-two cartridges for at least five injured. Not the kind of return you'd want under normal circumstance, but acceptable for our current situation.

I rushed to the roof and waited for his return, shouldering my rifle in case any vulture men made it through and I had a chance for a lucky shot. I was eventually greeted by Umma, landing heavily and huffing and puffing like an old steam engine. We went back to our defensive position together and I waited until he caught his breath before questioning him.

"How many did you take down?"

"Three...four maybe," he responded between breaths.

"Injured?"

"Seven...eight if I didn't kill...the last one."

I smiled in the dark and pulled out two gold eagles. "Unless you want to go up again, which I'd recommend against given how hard you're breathing." Probably not the best night to load up on haggis, but hindsight is 20/20. "I'd like to pay you for services rendered and have my binoculars back."

He gratefully accepted payment and handed the binoculars over. The darkness hid my rolling eyes—the lengths I had to go in order to avoid the sharing taboo! Umma would accept payment and equipage, but he wouldn't have accepted me just letting him use my binoculars—after all, he is a traditionalist at heart.

We remained in the dark room filled with braces against large rocks that never came for a full hour before calling it a night and parting ways. When I got to my room, I flopped into bed and turned on the vulture men's bug's live feed. Normally their hisses, caws, and throaty, guttural voices annoyed me, but tonight I enjoyed the noises of anger and chaos one flying pig with a gun had caused to their extortionist lives.

Chapter Fifteen

Fire In The Sky

Abigail was pleased as punch with Umma's bravery, and we had an impromptu celebration at breakfast that featured all three of the foods the food machine produced. Once we were all thoroughly stuffed, she pulled me aside and thanked me privately for my quick thinking.

Huh? Being thanked by Abigail?

After that unusual experience, my day brightened even more when the official count came in—four dead vulture men last night, which brought the grand total to fourteen, not to mention those wounded by Umma's pistol. That put a dent in their forces, and hopefully enough to give them pause and rethink their relationship with Deeplac. I hoped it would be enough for them to step back and leave us alone, but I certainly didn't expect it.

With the minimal damage from last night, the village resumed normal activity and I went about my daily chores. There were twelve new refugees from Oshkosh, two families of twin sisters. Once I cleared their medical examination, they were happily reunited with a cousin of theirs that arrived a few weeks earlier, and escorted to the kitchen for a late breakfast. Deeplac continued to grow quickly, regardless of our skirmish with the vulture men; the real combat was to our north and thankfully the wasteland raiders were focused on pushing further north to the heart of Oshkosh.

Next, to my mushrooms…but on the way to the basement, I changed my mind and sought out Gormond in the kitchen.

"You have any time to learn about the mushrooms?" I asked.

He put down a knife. "Now?"

"Yeah, I thought you'd like to learn sooner rather than later."

"Give me a few minutes and I'll meet you in the mushroom cellar?"

"Sounds good. I'll need to use the large soup pot and it'll take me that long to fill it up," I said, pointing at a huge fifty-gallon soup pot hanging over the center cutting station.

"It's all yours. We won't need it for a few more hours."

I unhooked the stainless steel pot and drew water from the well, filling it about two-thirds full. Deeplac has three wells: a small one in the kitchen, a larger one in the basement that is only accessible through the kitchen, and the largest in the outer courtyard. I hoisted the pot and carried the 250 lbs. of water down to the corner of the mushroom cellar.

Gormond joined me just as I was centering the pot over the rocket stove I'd fashioned out of ten cinder blocks to sterilize the water. There wasn't a need for a fire since he was there. He held his hand out about a foot from the pot and concentrated. Within a minute, the entire pot had reached boiling and he stopped concentrating.

"Impressive," I said with awe. I'd seen him heat objects before, but that didn't lessen the primal thrill of seeing the effects of fire where there was none.

"You should come by the smithy when I start up John's fire every morning," he shot back with a little swagger in his voice.

"How hot can you go?"

"Don't really know. I've gotten hot enough to turn metal white, but that takes several minutes and since I have to be pretty close to make it happen, I run the risk of burning myself."

I whistled in appreciation and showed him the sterilization process used to create the medium, that was then inoculated with the old medium possessing the mycelium of the oyster mushrooms. We did an entire bag in about fifteen minutes, and then I let him do one on his own.

"It'll take about two weeks for the mushrooms to start fruiting," I instructed, "and then you can harvest them every day for about four weeks before you have to start all over again. I've been getting about twenty to thirty pounds of mushrooms per square foot of bag. When you're done with a bag, hand it over to Herbert; he uses is as fertilizer where it thinks it's needed."

He looked at the room, counting the bags, and made a

rough estimate. "So, you mean this cellar should produce…"

"About half a ton of mushrooms per year," I finished for him. "I have space to double that before I'd have to move somewhere else."

The thought of a ton of mushrooms per year obviously pleased him. He was less excited at the daily ventilation needs of the mushrooms, but ten minutes turning a hand-cranked fan is a small price to pay.

"That's basically it," I summed. "The mushrooms do most of the work. It only becomes tricky when other types of fungi invade, but if you're sterilizing properly, that's a rare occurrence."

He thanked me for showing him how to take care of the mushrooms and returned to his work in the kitchen. It was nice to have someone interested in the production of my mushrooms. It was nice to know that someone knew how to take care of them and keep it going; even if I were to die on one of my missions, they would continue on without me. Yeah, I have parental feelings regarding fungi—sue me. It was a good—and tasty—return on just hay, and sure, the Dempster could turn any biomass into Scottish food, but how much Cullen skink could one community want? Gormond already did soup!

Curious what the tinkers were working on now that the food machine was operational, I stopped by Marilyn and Elissa's workshop to see what tech they'd uncovered. The pair were bent over a long bench, inspecting the dissected carcasses of the three police robots. Elissa smiled at me as I poked my head in. It wasn't her normal cheerful grin, but a devilish smirk. Before I could retreat, Marilyn looked up and called me out.

"About time you got here," the master tinker uttered dourly. "I've something I want to show you." I glanced at Elissa. What did I do? She gave me a "you'll see" expression.

I put on my best behavior before stepping through the threshold, and Marilyn escorted me to a corner and pulled out Conner's silvery gun from one of her many cabinets. She handed it to me; it was a lot heavier than I'd expected. Its cold, smooth silvery surface was absent of any triggers or buttons, except for the bottom of the grip, where one would place the magazine on a semi-automatic weapon. There was a slight depression at that point, but I didn't press it. I felt the weight of Marilyn's gaze, watching me examine it. I remained poker-faced under the scrutiny, but it made me nervous.

"I don't recognize it," I said neutrally.

"Given that you didn't recognize the egg or the battery, I'm not surprised. Press the depression," she said.

I followed her directions and the grip slipped open, revealing something within that I did recognize. "That's an empty klarklon compression chamber," I said. "Ha! That bastard Conner was bluffing the entire time."

Klarklon is a compressible gas that forms the plasma shot fired by my M1B, in conjunction with the power cell. I was probably the only one with any klarklon for miles—lord knows I had been looking for more since I arrived, as I have an extra power cell but only one cell of klarklon. I've been counting down the shots ever since I crawled out from my cryopod nearly two years ago. I shook my head now that I understood her irritation—she was worried she'd have to pay out the wazoo to get her hands on some, since I am loath to part with my M1B's fuel.

I looked up at Marilyn and her pursed lips were all the confirmation I needed.

"It would appear that Conner was a better liar than even I gave him credit for," she concurred, deigning to comment on the klarklon.

"So what's this do?" I asked.

"I don't know," she admitted. "It's driving me crazy!"

Out of the corner of my eye, I saw Elissa silently chuckle.

"It looks like a gun of some sort," I offered. The look I got in return could have stunned a crocophant.

"How about this: I insert my power and fuel cells into whatever this is and you can test it out one time without having to pay me for the fuel or power"—Marilyn had already started shaking her head, looking uncomfortable with the offer—"and in exchange, you let me use one of the community items in the future, no questions asked." I figured I would eventually need something, given my penchant for solving problems; others would have used the word "meddling," but there's no need to quibble over word choice.

"Done!" she accepted instantly, indicating that I failed in that exchange. Truth be told, I was just as interested as she was about what this silvery contraption did, and if that one M1B shot gave me access to something vitally needed in the future, I was willing to take that gamble. And since it was a barter for future use, it didn't even count as sharing.

I reached for my M1B, but she waved me away. "Not in here! We don't know what this is going to do, so we're going outside the walls." She thought a moment. "Let's go out to that firing range you set up and try it out there."

"Good idea," I agreed, even though it was raining. We went to the shooting range and she told me to stand back before she loaded the silvery object with the fuel and power cells. The instant she sealed the compression chamber, the object lit up. Lines of flashing blue, green, and red lights in various combinations and sigils illuminated the smooth sides. Marilyn and Elissa studied the glowing signs and muttered back and forth before reaching a conclusion, followed by a moment of shared laughter.

Well, that was a good sign, at least.

"Stonewall, don't forget our deal," she chided as she picked up the gun and tapped at various places along the barrel until the lights upon it turned a golden color. She then turned, and aimed at one of the bales of hay I'd set up fifty yards away. She simultaneously pressed a button on the top of the gun and one where a trigger would have been in a normal weapon, and a golden ray beamed out of the end. It connected with the hay bale, which immediately disappeared without a sound.

"Woah."

"Go check out the bale, Stonewall," Marilyn suggested.

I walked to where the bale used to be and found a lump of something golden lying on the ground. I picked it up after testing if it was hot. It was gold—about four or five ounces of it.

"It's gold?" I yelled out as I walked back.

"Yes," Elissa responded with mirth. "The 'gun' is actually a matter converter with a ranged effect. Most of them are chambers, not energy projectors."

I handed the lump of metal over to Marilyn. "I believe this is yours," I said ruefully. "You certainly got the best of that deal."

"That's how I prefer it," she said with a toothy grin, releasing and returning the fuel and power cells to me. I now had sixty-two shots left.

"That's an impressive gadget, but I'd rather have this"—I held up the M1B as I loaded the cells—"than five ounces of gold."

Marilyn shrugged. "To each their own, but it can do more than just gold; any metal or alloy can be created in limited amounts. If you ever find replacement fuel and power for your pistol, you may reach a different conclusion."

"It's a blaster, not a pistol," I corrected her as I twirled the M1B back into its holster. They rolled their eyes at me before returning their attention to the unpowered matter converter.

I headed back to my chamber to dry off and change out of my wet clothes. I had about six hours of recordings to process and Abigail wanted information as close to real-time as possibly to stay one step ahead of them. We didn't have a firm count, but with the current death tally at fourteen, we guessed they were down by a fourth to a third of their original numbers. Those kind of losses aren't shrugged off easily. Once an individual looks around and notices missing friends, they start to think they could be next. That kind of awareness spurs caution and fear, which only gets progressively worse.

The vulture men were in a state of confusion and one thing was certain: they absolutely hated us now, wishing only destruction, death, and fire upon us. You walked a fine line standing up to a bully, and that's exactly what they were. You had to beat them down enough to convince them to leave you alone, but if they lost too much face, they became implacable enemies, cowed enough to avoid direct confrontation, but who worked to ensure your downfall by any means available.

Refusing to be the object of their oppression and having them accept that change has always been my concern—that the vulture men lacked the ability to take such a blow to their collective ego. I'd spent months eavesdropping on them when they thought no one was listening—their internal organization and pride-centered community made a truly peaceful solution impossible, because there wasn't a way for Deeplac to stop paying tribute without making them lose too much face amongst themselves. Abigail's plan called for liberation from tribute, but my plan allowed Deeplac to stay free from vulture aggression permanently. Eventually, Abigail would have to set me loose to do what I knew needed to be done, but it wasn't today.

The vulture men planned another raid for tonight, which was consistent with the previous two nights; however, during this meeting, they were avoiding a direct discussion of tactics and strategy to the extent that I grew suspicious. Perhaps they were simply becoming overly cautious or maybe they suspected a traitor amongst them, given how easily we rebuffed their past two strikes. Their continued use of the communal room suggested they didn't suspect my bug, but the shift in conversation betrayed chaos in their community. They didn't know who or what to trust.

The only thing I could pick up were references to "unassailable heights" and a "trail of fire." I hadn't heard them use those phrases before, but I reported them to Abigail during dinner. Neither turn of phrase meant anything to her, but we both suspected they'd be flying higher than last night to avoid a certain flying pistol-packing pig man. The trail of fire made us nervous, so she decided to risk some riflemen at the gate towers in case they were planning something with their remaining horcs, perhaps an attempt to burn down the gates or some part of the walls?

While we talked, she asked if she could pay me a gold eagle to lease my binoculars to Umma for tonight's raid. I readily agreed and took her coin, promising to give them to Umma before nightfall. We parted ways, I grabbed my gear from my chamber, and settled in for tonight's raid in the room I'd been assigned to guard.

Umma joined me a quarter-hour before sunset and I gave him the binoculars. He was in a cheery mood, and his chest puffed proud after last night's heroism. From what I understood, he was the runt of his litter and been dealt a bad hand at birth, but he never lost his sense of optimism. This morning's small fete in celebration of his accomplishments meant a lot more to him than it would to most.

"Any word?" he asked once we'd secured the binoculars around his body. He didn't know how I seemed to know things before they happened, but he wasn't a dumb pig.

I shook my head. "Nothing really. Word on the street is they're coming in high tonight, so you may have quite the work out getting up to them." And with that sentence, I deflated him just a little. All his life, he'd been made fun of because his amazing gift of flight had so many limitations.

But you couldn't keep a good pig man down; he recovered quickly with a short laugh. "I'll have to be certain of my aim, then!"

"From last night's count, your aim's quite good," I bolstered his flagged feelings. "Hopefully daylight will reveal a few more of their feathery corpses."

He nodded and we sat in silence as the last rays of the setting sun turned the now-clear sky pink. Eventually, night came and Umma scanned the eastern horizon for the arrival of the vulture men. He'd been on watch for only a few minutes when Elissa surprised us with a visit, carrying her rifle over her shoulder and a small bag.

"Mind if I join you?" she asked.

"Sure, I don't mind. Stonewall?" Umma responded.

"Always a pleasure to have the best tinker in Deeplac as company," I teased. It was too dark to see her tufted ears flit, but in my mind they did.

"Ha, ha, funny man."

"One of my many talents," I crowed. "What's in the bag?"

"Marilyn thought it best I bring this for Umma," she said, pulling out a flare gun, the plastic orange one-shot variety. "She said that if you get in trouble, you could fire this off and maybe Stonewall could give you a rifle assist?" Her voice raised at the end, unsure if such was possible.

"I wouldn't be able to get off more than one shot, maybe two at most, but it could make a difference," I postulated.

"Thanks for this," Umma said, taking the pistol and wedging it into his belt. "I'll only use it if I'm in trouble and fleeing. Any cover you could provide would be well appreciated."

"Will do, pal."

Elissa joined me along the western wall while we waited. Umma kept scanning, but there wasn't any sign of the vulture men. We stayed silent for almost half an hour until we heard the sound of breaking glass and a flickering glow illuminated Umma against the eastern window.

"What the hell?" I said, rushing to the window.

I looked over the outer courtyard and saw the unmistakable trail of a Molotov cocktail—a fat center burst with a trail leading in the opposite direction of the throw.

"They're coming in from the north, not the east, and they are dropping firebombs. Elissa, you need to notify Abigail, if she doesn't already know, while Umma and I head toward the roof. It should be another fifteen minutes before their next attack and we need to be prepared," I ordered.

Elissa ran down the stairs to the communal room while we went up. Several patches of the roof were aflame, suggesting each individual vulture man was carrying several Molotov cocktails. But it wasn't just the roof that was on fire—some of the fields were burning. Umma and I looked at the flames, and we both understood that this avenue of attack must be stopped as quickly as possible.

Toward the north, I saw a few sparks of lights high in the air and I pointed them out, "Umma, look over there!"

He swiveled with the binoculars. "It's them. Flying in groups of five, carrying torches. They're really high up there, and they've brought two vulture dogs with them." He paused and his voice faltered at bit, "I don't think I'm going to be able to get that high."

I looked him square in the eyes. "You've got to try."

He mustered his courage and took to the air, little wings beating like mad. After he left, I circled the roof of the stronghold, counting the fires. It looked like each vulture man was carrying at least four incendiaries. The fires weren't very big and the soaking rain we'd had all day was surely putting a dent in their effectiveness, but in aggregate, over many runs, it was going to be a tremendous blaze if we didn't put a stop to this. I pulled out my rifle, hoping to get a bead off of their torches or cover Umma if he used the flare gun.

Through the scope, I could see the darkest shadows of the vulture men, but at this distance and with no real way to measure the wind, it would take a lucky shot to hit them. The best time for me to fire would be before they passed overhead, hopefully hitting them before they started lighting their incendiaries.

As they approached, I heard the first gunfire from Umma's pistol. Based off the muzzle flash, he was several hundred feet below them and I suspect he was straining to get that high. More shots rang out in quick succession, and the flare gun went off.

I put eye to scope and fired as quickly as I could, aiming for the dark silhouette of a vulture dog. I don't know if I hit. I moved the rifle upward toward the approaching flying torches and started firing rapidly. It was time to waste some valuable ammunition and try suppressive fire, the aerial edition. I chewed through twenty rounds before I confirmed a hit and kill. The falling vulture man slammed to the ground side-by-side with his torch, exploding in a small fireball of flaming alcohol.

The rest of the vulture men passed through, dropping their payload as they went, setting fire to fields and adding to the fire atop the stronghold. I was exposed in my position, but there was little I could do about that; I needed the full range of fire if I was going to pose a threat as they flew away. I believe I took out another, but I didn't get a fiery corpse to confirm the kill as they had already dropped their Molotov cocktails.

Flapping wings and huffing announced Umma's return. He was raked in several places, one particularly bad, and was covered in blood. I shouldered my rifle and—against his protestations—picked him up and carried him down to the communal room, adding to the confusion and fear of those within.

"Get me the first aid kit and some clean rags from the kitchen," I yelled at no one in particular as I made space for Umma in a protected corner. By the time I'd finished my initial assessment, the rags arrived. I staunched most of the blood in time for the first aid kit.

"You're going to be fine, my porcine friend," I reassured him.

"I got one vulture man, and one of the dogs before they got

to me. The second one hissed at me so bad it almost knocked me out, and then it was on me before I could escape. You must have got it with your rifle; otherwise I don't know how I got away. They fly a lot faster than I do," Umma said between winces as I cleaned out the wound with sterile saline and injected local anesthesia before sewed up the deep rake.

Over the din of the villagers taking cover inside the stronghold, I heard a ring of gunshots. Abigail must have come to the same conclusion I did—suppressive fire was the best solution, even if it did reduce a valuable resource. I made quick work closing Umma's wounds and bandaged them before I went out to continue my defense of Deeplac. The battle was over for my brave friend, but I was far from finished with the vulture men.

Chapter Sixteen

The Bigger They Are

The vulture men cut their attack short once we downed two more of their numbers. It took us three hours to put out all the fires and we lost an acre or two of grain in the struggle. Without the day's rain, we could have easily lost double or triple that amount, but the prospect of losing food was troublesome, considering our growing population.

Our saving grace was the vulture men's torches; if they could figure out a way to light their Molotov cocktails that didn't reveal their position to our rifles, there'd be no way we could effectively resist them. I convinced Abigail of this and she finally ordered me to implement my plan against the vulture men—I was to leave Deeplac by midafternoon, giving me a few hours to catch some sleep.

Before gathering my stuff, I stopped at Marilyn's workshop to pick up her metal gloves and had her respray me with anti-scent nanobots. It hadn't technically been a month since I was last sprayed, but both tinkers felt the risks were high enough to justify any potential waste. Where I was going, the last thing I needed was to have my scent return; both the horcs and the vulture men had a keen sense of smell, not to mention the night predators under the shattered moon. I consciously touched every piece of my equipment for a full minute to ensure the nanobots transferred, rendering all of my stuff scentless as well.

It was cool for a summer day, with thick clouds covering the sky and promising more welcome rain. If the vulture men followed precedent, tonight would bring another barrage, but if all went according to plan, it would be the last night of raids from the vulture men. I left amidst the sounds of the carpenters hurriedly making as many impromptu water buckets as possible; the water wouldn't put out the alcohol fires, but they did put out the fires left behind by them, and that was the best we could do without proper firefighting gear.

I silently wished them the best of luck and quickly left the gates behind me, making a beeline to the dense forest foliage and concealment against aerial observation. The vulture men have never used scouts before and there was nothing in the recordings to suggest they were doing such, but they were getting angrier and more desperate—a combination that made your enemy unpredictable—so caution and stealth were the guiding hand of my mission. Too much relied on it.

I'd traveled the route east of Deeplac to I-94 so many times in the past that I could do it in my sleep, so I redoubled my efforts to remain sharp. Familiarity dulls your senses and creates a patina of security over your brain. This vigilance revealed two buildings that had regenerated in the smaller ruins I had to travel through. If it had been a distraction of any other sort, I would have simply made a note of it and moved along, but you have to check out a regenerated ruin when you see it. The chance of a lucky find couldn't be passed over.

I explored the first regenerated ruin and found nothing of note. Some larger items and objects that would be okay scrapping, but nothing that grabbed me. The second ruin was more exciting, but again, nothing that would immediately help me on my mission. By cosmic irony, however, there was a full fire extinguisher in the second building. It would put me two hours behind to deliver it; I raised Abigail on the communicator so she could send a crew out to pick it up. It wasn't large enough to make a tactical difference, but it was far from worthless, and she'd want it if the vulture men returned with more fire.

With that brief diversion finished, I marched back into the forest and then up some thick vines to the middle level of I-94. I kept to the center of the massive plascrete highway as I moved south, reducing the likelihood of a chance encounter. The center of the highway was a thick barricade about six feet tall and littered with drain pipes, most of which were broken. The falling rain coated the area and a thick green moss covered everything; in some places it was more than a foot thick, under which rested a loamy soil. Its smell was not unpleasant, and I wondered—not for the first time—if it were edible, hoping I would never have cause to find out.

I eventually arrived where Diana and I had previously

camped. The moss was thoroughly disrupted and the rough chairs we'd created were knocked down. I readied my rifle as I moved in for a closer examination. It didn't take me long to discover a few large feathers—vulture men, I presumed. With our observation perch discovered, I hightailed it farther south. It was unlikely they put the location on their own watch, considering they'd gone to some lengths to destroy it, but I didn't want to hang around to find out.

I traveled until I got to the collapsed portion of the lower deck of I-94, about a mile south of the observation point. I had used this section to descend to the ground in the past, and the upper level was still intact, shielding me from aerial view. It was still a few hours until sunset, so I improvised a small resting seat out of moss and leaned against one of the massive pillars, eyes facing the slope down. It was unlikely I'd encounter any fauna since I was scentless, but that was no reason to let down my guard. I pulled out my adaptive ghillie suit and spread it over me like a blanket, so that I blended into the background—I was just an odd lump of gray plascrete and moss until you were almost upon me.

Time dragged for hours, but eventually day became night, and I started moving east while the sun was setting. I was about a mile south of the Lancaster Building and five miles west, and I moved under the cover of darkness, alternating between quick movement for fifty yards and minutes of stillness and silence to assess my surroundings. It was tiring, but it worked.

About half a mile into the trip, I stopped in a bricked crevice created by the fallen corner of a mid-nineteenth-century building. Not much of it remained except the corner, and I'd chosen it for the cover it provided. I waited, listening, and was about to move on when I heard an unmistakable noise indicating I wasn't alone—footsteps. I tuned in and identified three pairs, which could be deceptive given the ability for multiple-limbs among sentients beneath the shattered moon.

This mission had a strict no-engagement policy. I must avoid alerting the vulture men or the horcs to my presence, meaning that I should take all measures to remain unseen, and if seen, silence my foes before they could raise an alarm. This put my rifle off-limits, although I brought it with me for later. That left me with my M1B, which only made as much noise as dropping a basket of fries into hot oil. My knife was a last resort; I'd rather not be that close to enemy combatants.

I bided my time quietly and my patience was rewarded: three horcs rounded the bend of the block cattycorner to the one in which I was hidden. There was no way to tell if they were associated with the vulture men. They walked along the middle of the street, passed by me, and then continued on for another block before turning south. Regardless of their larger place in my schemes, I'd avoided their detection.

I waited for another two minutes before moving again, slowly creeping my way through the darkness toward the Lancaster Building. I wanted to approach from the northeast corner and allotted another two hours before I got to the building, leaving me two hours to perform my mission and an hour to escape before sunrise.

Once I reached the desired corner of the building, I took a brief breather to release some of the tension of the past few hours, readying myself for the next part. I donned Marilyn's gloves and tied them tight at the wrist with a modified slip knot—the more weight on the knot, the tighter it pulled around my wrist until I pulled the end of the string to release the knot. Using my natural abilities and the power of the gloves, I scaled eleven stories of the Lancaster Building expeditiously until I reached the skeletonized part of the structure. I breathed a sigh of relief when I arrived; hanging on the corner of the building was like standing on top of a hill—even with my adaptive ghillie suit, you'd see my silhouette.

After catching my breath, I got to work. I shed the ghillie suit and used it for cover as I lit up my plasma torch beneath it, cutting partway through the corner support beam I'd just crawled up. Under the suit, the plasma's light was diffused, rendering it into something indistinguishable from a patch of phosphorescent lichen. It would stand out if you were looking at the area, but if you were looking away, it wouldn't be enough to draw your attention. Whenever I could, I placed the beam between the torch and the northwest; the vulture men would be flying in and out tonight and keeping the beams between us decreased my chances of being detected.

In quick succession, I cut through every beam. It was a steel-frame construction, and I had a lot of them to get through. I varied the depth of my cuts—the first cut went through seventy percent of the support, the second cut went through fifty percent. If the engineers had done their work properly, the building would stay upright under my plasma cutter's assault. This wasn't a suicide mission, after all.

Once I'd cut through the beams, the dangerous work was done. My chances of being detected dropped to nigh zero once the cutter stop shining. I put it away and pulled out the explosives I'd obtained from the basement of the old gun shop. Even though a hundred feet should do the trick, I'd brought all two hundred feet of flexible linear shaped charge since I lacked det cord to connect the charges. I wove it in six interlinked and angled sections, and placed a timed detonator on each section, set to explode two hours after sunrise.

There wasn't much I could do to hide my work, as the vulture men had stripped this floor clean. I relocated what incidental debris I could find to make the connections less obvious. On the off chance that the vulture men took note of the charges, I set up a radio detonator as backup. Marilyn had used some of her goo to extend the range out to ten miles, which was orders of magnitude greater than I thought I needed, but she told me that was the only way it was going to happen, so I'd yielded to her stipulation.

I called in my success to Abigail via the communicator and

descended the building the same way I'd gone up. I maneuvered my way back, oscillating between a quick decisive hustle and quiet stillness, undetected by horcs, vulture men, and vulture dogs. It was a textbook mission and I was still pleased with how smoothly it had gone down by the time I returned to my observation spot on I-94.

This is the part they never tell you about in regard to being an operative—if you've done your job right, it's largely uneventful. You shouldn't have a big fight or have to use a rolled-up magazine as an impromptu weapon. They shouldn't even know that you had been there until their fate was already sealed. It's frustrating, because you never get the satisfaction of watching your enemy's eyes when he realizes you've bested him, and the work is only judged by its effect. It's not a game, and those who treat it as such eventually die.

I would have loved some sleep, but I had to keep eyes on the building in case the vulture men discovered my meddling and I had to use the radio detonator. An hour after sunrise, I was joined by a squad of twenty Deeplacers with rifles. They were led by Grendel, who had to have his rifle modified to suit his giant hands, as well as Zew and Diana, who were always game for anything dangerous. A few of them were battered and bandaged but most were uninjured, if a little bruised and smoky.

I turned to Grendel. "How much damage did they do?"

The giant grunted. "More than we hoped, but only a little

more than we'd expected."

"Any causalities?" I asked with dread.

"Only theirs," he said stoically. "Everything they destroyed can be replanted and repaired." I smiled and I could have sworn I saw the corner of Grendel's mouth turn up slightly. "Did everything go as planned?"

"Everything's in place. They haven't detected anything yet. Take a look if you want." I offered the binoculars to him. He declined.

He looked grimly toward the tall building in the distance. "Everyone take up a spot along the barricade. We need to ensure that any vulture man or dog that makes it out of the explosion doesn't decide to vent their disappointment upon Deeplac."

The squad lined up behind the barricade, taking a knee on the thick moss. It was unlikely that very many vulture men would survive and even more so that they'd decide to attack Deeplac immediately afterward, but we'd prepared for that risk. Mostly the squad was here to clean up once the building was down.

Speaking of which…

"We've got ten minutes to go," I announced.

The tension and excitement was high. None of the sentients had ever witnessed anything of this magnitude, and when the explosions went off, we watched the building soundlessly start to collapse. They jumped when the shockwave hit us with its resounding roar, and down the Lancaster Building went, sending up a massive cloud of dust in its stead.

We watched the skies for vengeful survivors, but all we saw was the ash settle to the ground. I pulled out the communicator and was about to hail Abigail when I felt a heavy hand on my shoulder.

"Let me tell her," the hulking commander spoke softly, and I placed the tech in his massive hand.

Epilogue

It took hours for the dust to settle from the fallen Lancaster Building, and we upon I-94 celebrated the destruction with sips from shared flasks of whiskey brought for this purpose; not enough to dampen our senses, but just enough to mark the moment of Deeplac's freedom from the vulture men. Once the dust was clear, we descended to the ground and headed toward the once-great building.

Along the way, we encountered a few horcs who had escaped the carnage, but as soon as we'd taken a few down, the others scattered eastward, fleeing before the sound of our rifles. We marched in the hot sun for a few miles, carefully watching the ruins around us before reaching the giant mound of rubble we'd created. It was looting time. This initial grab was to pick up the surface finds; there would be a long and thorough scavenging operation conducted over the coming months.

I teamed up with Zew and Diana, heading toward the farthest fallen rubble—the best stuff would be found among the remains of the penthouse. We were joined by several other teams who had the same idea and our opinion proved accurate. The first thing we found was a scattered pile of gold eagles which we split amongst ourselves, each getting six after accounting for Deeplac's take.

"Even if we don't find anything else, I think I'll be fine with this," Zew said, clinking the coins together.

Diana smiled in agreement as she wrapped the coins into a rag, twisting it around each coin so that they didn't make noise when they hit each other. "I agree, but not from a lack of trying. Let's keep looking," she addressed both of us. "The other groups are spreading out here. Let's move to the east and sweep that area before anyone else gets to it."

We hustled around the edge of the rubble, keeping our eyes open for anything of interest. Along the way to the east, we picked up assorted items of lesser value, filing the extra bags we always carried with us. By the time we got to the farthest part of the rubble, we didn't have a lot of space left, but we kept searching...you could always trade out a lesser-value item for something better.

We split up to cover more area, Zew and I on the edges and Diana clambering around the center. It was less than a minute when she squeaked—it had to be good if it made Diana shriek like Elissa.

"Hey Zew, come look at this," Diana called to the mohawked wastelander; he was closer to her than I was.

"What you got?" he queried, climbing up to her picking area.

"I don't know, but it's silvery like the flying egg," she replied, handing over a silver sphere roughly the size of a softball.

"It's warm," he said suspiciously.

"It cools down. Wait."

"That's strange; now it doesn't feel warm at all."

I crawled over to get a look at what they'd found. Zew cradled it in both of his hands, flipping it around. It was perfectly smooth and composed of the same material as the egg, the broadcast battery, and Conner's silvery matter converter. So far, everything made of that material was quite the find.

"Nice find, Diana! We don't have to know what it is since I bet Marilyn will, and you'll get a nice price for it from her or the council if they want it for their own," I said.

Zew handed it over to me, "Here. See how it warms and then cools."

I took the silvery softball from him. It felt warm in my hands but the temperature rapidly escalated until I instinctively dropped it to avoid getting burned.

"Stonewall! What the hell?" Diana yelled at me.

"It kept getting hotter and it felt like it was going to burn me," I defended myself.

Her anger turned off like a switch. "Sorry," she apologized, reaching to pick up the sphere. She tentatively touched it and quickly pulled away. "Yeah, it's really hot now. Did you do anything?" she queried.

Before I could answer her question, a full-color hologram of a lovely human lady dressed in a prim pink suit projected out of the sphere. Behind her was a massive gleaming city rising out of the desert. "Congratulations! You and your family have won an all-expenses paid vacation to exciting Las Vegas, where you'll experience two weeks of once-in-a-lifetime luxury in the hotel penthouse of the opulent Las Vegas Phoenix Casino."

The hologram panned along the skyline of the Las Vegas of my future, pausing dramatically on a massive towering structure emblazoned with a flashing neon phoenix that lit up the night. The perky-voiced lady continued, "A penthouse of beauty and palatial extravagance, of one thousand and one follies, a penthouse that crowns the largest casino in the world. You'll enjoy luxury as you've never imagined!"

The hologram flickered and slowly died away to the diminishing sound of tinny classical music. Diana reached down and tentatively touched the silvery softball. "It's cool now," she said, lifting it out of debris.

"Well. That was strange," I said.

THE END

Stonewall will next appear in *Stonewall Against Las Vegas.*